D0837855

HIGH MILE RIDER

McGinley was a loner, a natural drifter who had learned to survive the hard way. So it came as no surprise to find himself on the run from a 'hanging-crazed' sheriff, and accused of a violent killing he didn't commit. But when mistaken identity and gold-hungry gunslingers are added to his troubles, McGinley takes to the snowy mountain trails in a bid to stay ahead of the bullets. Now death is never more than the next crack of ice away.

JACK REASON

HIGH MILE RIDER

Complete and Unabridged

LINFORD
Leicester

First published in Great Britain in 2001 by
Robert Hale Limited, London

First Linford Edition
published 2002
by arrangement with
Robert Hale Limited, London

The moral right of the author
has been asserted

British Library CIP Data

Reason, Jack
    High mile rider.—Large print ed.—
Linford western library
1. Western stories
2. Large type books
I. Title
823.9′14 [F]

ISBN 0–7089–9949–2

Published by
F. A. Thorpe (Publishing)
Anstey, Leicestershire

Set by Words & Graphics Ltd.
Anstey, Leicestershire
Printed and bound in Great Britain by
T. J. International Ltd., Padstow, Cornwall

This book is printed on acid-free paper

This for L.B.
May she stay sharp-eyed!

1

He was cheating death for the second time in less than a week.

Another few steps, another deep breath and the gut determination to make it to the cabin, and he would be through the door and into shelter. And then these godforsaken mountains, the snow, the ice, the biting wind of a Colorado winter and the hanging-crazed sheriff somewhere on his tail, could go to Hell.

He would have beaten the odds — again.

He waited, near exhausted, his body slumped, heavy and half frozen, against the bulk of the tree, blinked on iced lids, could almost hear the crack of his frosted stubble, raised a soft growl from the pit of his stomach and forced the life back to his numbed legs.

The step was slow and painful, his

1

boots like rocks under the weight of snow, the effort little more than a shuffle, but he was moving and the cabin, black as a bruise on the fading light, sometimes only a blur in the swirl of the snowfall, that much closer.

'Shift!' he grunted, and willed the boot to lift.

One step, two, three . . .

It had taken less than a dozen in the stroll from the street to the boardwalk and the saloon-bar batwings five days back to change his life and bring him to this.

He should have ridden clear of the town of Remarkable when he had had the chance, kept moving west, disregarded his hunger, his tiredness, the thoughts of a soft feather-bed, clean sheets and a roof over his head for the night. He should have stayed with what he knew, what he had always known: the trail, the dust and dirt, flea-chewed blankets and a ceiling of stars.

He should have stayed plain, ordinary, no fuss, quiet-spoken Jim McGinley, the man with the worn saddle and patched bags, one horse and a bedroll, a trusted Colt, broad-brimmed hat, seedy pants, down-at-heel boots, frayed shirt and fading waistcoat. A man who barely raised a second glance, broad shouldered and weathered, but who carried the marks of every one of his thirty-two years.

'Just call me McGinley,' was the normal extent of his conversation, though the set and depth of his pale-blue eyes tended to see and say a whole lot more.

Jim McGinley was a travelling man — some might mistakenly have said a drifter — forever on the move, never settling, always content to see the distance between himself and the last place he had slept lengthening to uneventful miles. He was never anywhere longer than suited and came and went at his own bidding.

Until the town of Remarkable.

He had sensed, almost smelled, something was wrong the moment he had hitched his mount at the rail

3

fronting The Hopeful Dollar saloon and made his slow, weary way to the 'wings and the welcoming sounds of the bar beyond them.

The day across the empty mesa had been long, cloud-heavy and rainswept on the first of the Fall winds, not one in which to relish the open spaces and the prospects of a slow, easy trail to a quiet campfire and the tang on the night of fresh brewed coffee. No, he had decided, not that sort of day at all; rather one to cover the miles fast, hold to the main trail and hope for the sight of town smoke long before dark.

He had been lucky, he had found Remarkable. Leastways, it had seemed like luck.

The raised voices had halted him at the 'wings . . . 'So what yuh sayin' there, mister? Yuh callin' me a liar? Yuh sayin' as how I cheated?'

'I'm sayin' as how yuh dealin' that hand from a stacked deck. You count them cards out, fella. See for yourself.'

'Anybody else reckon for this deck

4

bein' stacked? You reckon so — you there, behind that black beard?'

'Me? I didn't see nothin', mister. I ain't even playin' cards!'

'Yuh hear that? He didn't see nothin'.'

'He ain't sittin' here, is he? He ain't watchin' and seein' what I'm seein'.'

'So you're still callin' me out as a cheat. That the way of it?'

'I'm tellin' yuh — '

'Well, I ain't for bein' told nothin' by the likes of you, fella. Specially not by you. This deal's fair up and true. Anybody says different, they got Chems Parton to reckon to.'

McGinley had frowned at the mention of the name. Chems Parton . . . The same Parton he had seen billed as Wanted out Tavistock way? The same fellow they reckoned for one of the guns in the Belle Junction hold-up?

He had pushed open the 'wings with the fingers of one hand already flexing over the butt of his holstered Colt.

★ ★ ★

The squeak of tight, dry hinges, the creak of a floorboard to the scuff of a boot, sounds that were suddenly exaggerated in the tension of a smoke and liquor-hazed saloon bar, had been all that were needed to spark Chems Parton's nerves.

McGinley had watched the man turn, Colt in hand, a wild, excited look in his eyes, and drawn instinctively on his own piece at the sight of a barrel pointing his way.

The player protesting the honesty of Parton's dealing had pushed his chair from the table and come unsteadily to his feet, his own gun still holstered at his side. McGinley had given him a quick glance, flicked his gaze back to Parton, then to a man lurking in the shadows at the rear of the bar.

A Colt spat — the man in the shadows — the shot winging high and wide to the left, shattering a main window fronting the street.

A bar girl screamed. Another swore violently and crashed a bottle across the head of a groping drunk. The barman smothered a jug of his best whiskey out of sight. A fancy waistcoated man heeled a half-smoked cigar, reached for his hat, only to see it crushed under foot in a mêlée of suddenly swearing, fist-swinging drinkers.

More screams. More curses. More crashes.

And then another blazing shot.

This time the man facing Chems Parton had fallen forward, his already blood-soaked hands clutching his gut.

Parton had sneered, laughed raucously, grabbed a bottle of whiskey and splashed the liquor into his mouth.

Somebody had torn a bar-girl's dress to send her scurrying half naked for the stairs to the balcony rooms. She had tripped, scrambled, been hurled back across the bar and into McGinley's side.

It was at that moment, with McGinley floundering for his balance against the spinning girl, conscious of the need to keep a grip on his Colt and one eye on Chems Parton, that the Winchester had barked from the boardwalk and the batwings crashed open under the pounding bulk of a bull-necked sheriff and a pair of snarling, Colt-wielding deputies.

2

Somebody had yelled: 'Hank Green's been shot! He's dead! Right here, damn yuh. Right under our noses. Sonofa-goddamn-bitch!'

Chems Parton had disappeared. Drinkers stood blank-eyed, open-mouthed. Girls sobbed. The fancy waistcoated man rubbed inanely at the specks of blood splattered across his clothes. The barman poured himself a generous measure and sank it in one.

The half-naked girl who had been hurled across the bar, clawed and crawled to the nearest shadowed corner and curled herself to a ball.

The sheriff slapped a fat heavy hand on McGinley's shoulder, at the same time prodding the barrel of the Winchester deep into his ribs.

'My good friend, Hank Green's lyin'

dead there and you're the only man in this bar with a gun in his hand, mister,' he growled, his breath like a hot wind across McGinley's neck. 'Now my figurin' tells me that makes you a prime candidate for the hangin' rope I got back there in my office.' The barrel prodded deeper. 'So happens we ain't had ourselves a decent hangin' in this town in weeks, and I do enjoy a decent hangin',' leered the lawman. 'Town folk feel the same. Oh, yessir, do they! Get kinda hungry for it. Know what I mean? Like feedin' a habit, eh? So you just drop that piece right where yuh stand, yuh hear, and me and my boys'll make sure yuh have a safe walk to the jail.' McGinley could almost feel the man's sneer slithering across his neck. 'Let's move, shall we?'

If McGinley had learned anything in his years of ensuring his survival and staying alive, it was never to argue with a crazy-faced sheriff with an obvious fetish for ropes and hangings.

It was time, he had concluded, to be

clear of the town of Remarkable. No protesting his innocence to the sheriff, of describing what had really happened in the dispute between Hank Green and Chems Parton, of seeking the support of the others in the bar.

None of this.

Just get the hell out, through the batwings to the street in one decisive rush, mount up, stay close and low on his mount and ride like the wind in a twister.

It had taken less than two minutes to do just that. But he had not reckoned for the trouble sitting tight on his tail.

* * *

It had been close on an hour of hard, unbroken riding on the main trail west, with the light fading fast and the night beginning to clamour all round him, before McGinley had become aware of the thunderous beat of the chasing posse fast closing behind him.

Say one thing for the hanging-happy

sheriff, he had thought through the thinnest of wry smiles, he was not for giving up easily. But that was as far as McGinley's view of the lighter side was to stretch. The situation was not for being dismissed or ridden away from on some grunt of encouragement to his already weary mount.

Fact was, he had concluded, reaching the straggle of an outcrop of pine, he was facing only one real option: to leave the main trail, take to the cover of the trees to the foothills and trust that he could find a track to deeper hiding in the mountains.

Not an exactly welcoming prospect at this time of the year with the first snows dusting the high peaks and slopes, with the barest of supplies, no gun, a tired mount and an ice-edged wind already whipping round him.

No prospect, but a choice that might be sufficient to cool the venom of the tracking riders.

★   ★   ★

The snowstorm had hit soon after noon on the second day of McGinley's climb into the mountains.

It had threatened in darkening, thickening cloud since first light. The wind, swirling and buffeting from the north-east had strengthened relentlessly driving the snows to an enveloping curtain until, within an hour, McGinley had been forced to seek what scant shelter he could find among the rocks.

So what now of the sheriff and his hungry posse, he had wondered, as the morning had settled to snowswept hours where only the howling wind broke the silence? He must be similarly holed up, men and mounts tucked tight into whatever cover had come to hand, but for how long, and would they resume the chase when the storm eased?

Or would they cut their losses, leave the mountains to the worsening weather and McGinley to whatever frozen fate awaited him? Maybe somebody would get to telling the truth of the shooting before Chems Parton had crossed the territorial border and faded from sight like a shadow into night. Maybe.

There had been no way of knowing the time of day or how many hours had passed when McGinley finally stirred and creaked and crackled from the sheltering rocks like an insect emerging from a chrysalis. The snowfall had remained steady, blanketing the mountains until the only protrusions were the taller, thicker masses of rock and bleak fingers of pine.

He had waited, listening and watching, for just long enough to be certain that the sheriff and his guns were not close or approaching, then pushed on, every slithering, frozen few yards seeming like a mile.

Another day, another night . . . more than one? He had no idea and was within a spit of not caring, of almost willing the men tracking somewhere behind him to catch up and either put an end to it right there, or drag him back to the warmth of a jail cell, when he had stumbled, more dead than alive, into the taller, thicker stand of pines and seen the cabin.

Again, he had waited, one hand flat on a pine trunk, the other twisted into a grip on the reins of his near exhausted mount trailing behind him. His body, wrapped in his bedroll blanket, was caught in spasms of shaking and shivering, his sight blurred under what seemed like a coating of ice, his breath tight and choking.

But there was no doubt in his mind as to what he was seeing. The cabin was there, real, probably deserted — who cared, anyhow? — a safe shelter against the weather if nothing else.

To hell with the crazy sheriff and his hanging-crazed posse, this was as far as McGinley was going. He had cheated the prospect of death once, he could do it again.

Just a few more steps . . .

3

McGinley blew what little warm breath he could summon across his fingers as he settled his mount in the roughly-hewn lean-to at the side of the cabin then turned his dazed attention to the door.

Was it locked? Had the home been long abandoned? There was nothing to be seen through the frosted window. Maybe he would be forced to break in. Who had chosen to live out here in the remote mountains anyway: a hunter, fur trader, a hermit? Supposing he was on his way back to the place. Supposing the sheriff and his posse knew of the cabin and its owner.

He laid a frozen hand to the door latch and prayed. The supposing was over if he wanted to stay alive.

The door creaked and grated open, releasing a waft of dust-laden, musty air that seemed to clamour at McGinley's face as if warding him off. He blinked, brushed aside a skein of cobwebs and stepped into the dark living area, closing the door firmly on the still falling snow and whipping wind.

He waited, blinking on the thin shaftings of light that probed the darkness, his widening stare taking in the few shapes he could identify: wall ahead of him, stone fireplace, cooking pots, tools, logs; two chairs and a table. He blinked again. Been a while since anyone had eaten here, but there were clean plates, a tin mug, glasses and what looked gloriously like a half-bottle of whiskey.

McGinley reached for the drink with icicle fingers on a shaking hand, curled them round the bottle and drew it towards him. But it was a long minute before he had managed to remove the cork and gulp on the liquid, its warmth coursing through his body like a dosing of liquid sunlight.

He shuddered, wiped the back of his

hand across his mouth, replaced the bottle and returned to his identification of the shapes around him. Pair of boots close to the window — the fellow could afford two pairs, pondered McGinley? — quality coat and hat hanging from a nail; ropes, a belt, box of cartridges. Ammunition could only mean . . . He stepped closer, his gaze tight and concentrated, moving quickly left to right until — he had it! There, propped in the corner, a Winchester.

Things were getting better, he smiled thinly to himself.

He turned, ran a hand over the scrubbed table. Maybe the place had not been deserted that long, he thought. There was dust, sure enough, some cobwebs, there was a smell of emptiness but perhaps no more than days old and already fading on the icy cold.

Place needed a fire, warmth, light. He would search out blankets for his mount, himself, check if there was any food. Fellow seemed to have enough of

18

everything. There were sure to be provisions. In fact, now he came to thinking closely on it . . .

Why was there a pair of boots, a quality coat and hat, a rifle, ammunition? Was whoever lived here some wealthy hunter who believed in having two of everything to survive remoteness?

McGinley shrugged and grunted on his thoughts, uncorked the bottle again and relished the life-giving warmth of the whiskey. It could be, of course, he mused on, that the fellow . . .

He slammed the bottle to the table, crossed the room to the smaller door that he supposed led to a sleeping area, and was already pushing it open when he sensed the new smell and felt the sole of his boot slide into the spread of congealed blood.

★　★　★

The man had been dead some time, shot through the head, close range,

19

probably a Colt, but there were no signs of a fight or even a scuffle. The killer had been someone the man had known. His partner, wondered McGinley, would that explain the two of everything? Had there been a dispute here, a row that had erupted and ended in a violent death?

But who was the dead man?

A closer inspection of the body revealed nothing in the way of an identity, save that McGinley put him at around thirty years of age, balding, a tough, well weathered look to his skin, with heavily calloused hands. Maybe been a wrangler or lumberman at some stage in his life.

But not out here in a cabin high in the Colorado mountains. So how and why and when had he arrived; alone or with his partner?

Hell, thought McGinley, covering the body with a blanket, did it matter? Nothing to be done for the fellow now. And in any case, he had his own problems: the weather, saturated clothes, a horse in need of attention, and a hang-'em-high minded sheriff and his posse sitting somewhere out there just waiting on the snowfall easing.

The dead man had gone miserably to his Maker, but gone nonetheless, and McGinley was not in the business at this moment of righting that particular wrong.

What the fellow had left behind, however, was a different matter.

With his mount finally settled in the lean-to as best he could organize, McGinley had turned his attention to rummaging through the contents of the cabin and the dead man's personal belongings for whatever he figured he would need for a long trek over the mountains.

And trek it was going to be. He had no choice, not if he was taking the persistence of the sheriff seriously — and he was doing that, no mistake! Minute the weather eased, the lawman would be mounted up again and back on the trail. He might even know of the cabin; might be reckoning on his man holing-up here a while, resting, thawing out, sleeping . . .

No chance of that, worst thing he could do. Once asleep here he could be certain of waking roped to the back of a horse with a cell and the hangman's noose his next and last prospect.

He would be gone just as soon as he had changed into a set of warm, dry clothes, eaten whatever he could find that was edible, packed the mount with anything useful, loaded the Winchester and could see at least a horse length ahead of him. No matter what the weather, he would face it, get clear, climb higher, cross the range wherever he could find a creek or gulch that was passable, hold to the pine stands where he found them and eventually, given a snatch of luck, reach one of the mining towns on the lower reaches.

How far the sheriff would track him, or for how long, he had no notion, but given the miles, maybe some better weather and, by then, a much reduced posse, the odds might be more equally spread.

He could only hope.

★ ★ ★

The snowfall had eased to a scattering drift, the wind backed and the light strengthened sufficient to smudge the darkness to a dull grey, when McGinley finally left the cabin wearing the dead man's quality coat and hat, his polished boots, clean buckskin pants and warm woollen shirt.

Had he had the money he would have been fair-minded and left the cabin man a payment for his help and hospitality. As it was, he was clean out of cash.

And the cabin man was still very dead.

4

McGinley hugged the cover and darker sprawl of pines for as long as he could and until they finally petered out and he was forced to the tracks twisting to the higher peaks. But, he consoled himself, the weather had eased to no more than a brisk, freezing wind; he was warmer, drier, his mount moving at a steady pace, and there had been no sight or sounds of the posse.

Maybe they had given up against the biting cold and snowfall, or lost the trail, or simply reckoned the terrain too difficult and the mountain trails no prospect.

Or maybe, like some long shadow, they would reach out with the light.

McGinley resolved he would trail steadily north while ever the weather and going permitted, following the track he had picked up that seemed to be heading between the bulks of two ranges. Given any luck, he might find himself with an easier passage than looked to be the case in any direction he cared to scan at the moment; little more than snow, frozen rocks, lean tree cover and always the threatening menace of winter clouds skimming the highest peaks.

Rough, uncompromising country; tough going; no place for man or beast, save when there happened to be the sheriff of Remarkable hunting you down. Then it was the only place to be.

★ ★ ★

He had trailed on until noon and beyond without pause, climbing at first higher and, to his nervous concern, ever more exposed against the bright, burning sunlight; then, by mid afternoon, into the shadow-filled safety of a reach of pines. It was here, with the wind backing to a slow, mournful moan and the fresh snowfall frisking in flakes as broad and slow as leaves, that he halted, dismounted, spoke softly, comfortingly to the mount, and delved deep into his saddlebag for the whiskey taken from the cabin.

Time to reflect, take in his position and prospects, reckon on the next move and the tracks to be followed while the weather held and the light stayed good. Time too, he thought, to watch, listen, detect the slightest hint of the sheriff and his guns still following. And time, not the least, for the warmth and cheer of a dead-man's whiskey.

He had the bottle in his hand, uncorked and was lifting it to his lips when the single shot from a steady, levelled Winchester cracked across the silence and he was left with no more than the neck of the bottle in his grip and the liquor splashed into his stubble.

The mount bucked and snorted. McGinley flinched but stood his ground and turned slowly, almost casually, his gaze narrowing, to face the source of the shot, the shattered neck of the bottle still in his hand.

A bear of a man smothered in the depths of a long fur coat, a broad-brimmed hat pulled low and tight so that only the gleam of his eyes and the cynical leer at his lips were visible.

'Bet yuh'd been droolin' on the thought of that, eh, mister?' croaked the man, the rifle still levelled from his shoulder, the aim steady. 'Shame, but I ain't much for the sins of liquor m'self, so mebbe done yuh a real favour there, eh?' His gaze tightened and darkened. 'Don't matter none. You're sober and alive, and that's how we want yuh.' He paused a moment. 'This our man, Wilbur?'

The man he addressed by name, taller and leaner, but similarly shrouded in the folds of a long fur coat, the slouching brim of his hat twitching on the whip of the wind, the reins to two horses tight in his hand, grinned and clicked his tongue. 'You're right, Mr Coon,' he grinned, 'this is our man. No mistakin' — Frank Boyd as ever was. We found him.'

McGinley continued to stare, still gripping the remains of the bottle, his other hand soft on his mount's neck. He swallowed quietly, licked on a flurry of snowflakes at his lips and wondered fearfully how far and high the echo of the rifle shot had drifted across the mountains. And, just who, in the name of tarnation, was Frank Boyd?

Mr Coon spat over the barrel of the Winchester. 'We been waitin' on yuh, Boyd,' he mouthed carefully, his gaze glinting. 'Two whole days. Took yuh time, didn't yuh?'

McGinley dropped the broken bottle to the snow and scuffed his boot across it. 'Looks like yuh might be waitin' a whole while longer, fella.' He smiled. 'I ain't Boyd. Name's McGinley.'

Wilbur twitched and tittered. 'Oh, sure. And the moon's apple pie, mister!' He clicked his tongue nervously. 'We heard say as how yuh might be travellin' under another name.'

'Incognito,' clipped Mr Coon.

'Yeah, that too,' added Wilbur on

another click. 'Your style, ain't it?'

'I haven't a snowball's hope in hell of understandin' a word of what you're sayin',' sighed McGinley.

Mr Coon lowered the rifle across his body. 'Yuh wanna call y'self McGinley, yuh go right ahead and do just that. I ain't for stoppin' yuh. As far as I'm concerned you're Frank Boyd. Good enough. Sorry about the bottle, but, like I say, me and Wilbur ain't much for liquor and we need yuh sober. Clear, clean-headed. Yuh got it?'

'Now, look,' began McGinley again, 'I ain't — '

'So yuh keep sayin',' shrugged Mr Coon. 'Tell him, Wilbur. Spell it out.'

Wilbur grinned and flicked at the wayward hat brim. 'You're Boyd. Ain't no doubtin' to that. Them clothes — the boots, buckskin pants, that fancy mountain coat, and the rifle yuh got scabbarded there — ain't no mistakin' takin' them. They're Boyd's. You, mister, are Frank Boyd, one and the same like we were told to look for.'

29

'So you've never actually met this fella Boyd?' said McGinley.

'Not personally we ain't,' grunted Mr Coon. 'Ain't been the need 'til now, has there? No point — not 'til yuh agreed to help the boys back there.'

'The boys?' frowned McGinley, his head beginning to spin on the sight of the men and their crazy notion as to who he was. 'Who the hell are the boys?'

'Say this for yuh, mister,' grinned Wilbur, 'yuh sure don't give nothin' away, do yuh? Ain't nobody goin' to fool you. Fake Morgan said as much. Said as how yuh were nobody's dumb head. You recall that, Mr Coon?'

'I do indeed, Wilbur. I do indeed.'

'Hold it — hold it right there,' soothed McGinley, gesturing with raised arms in spite of the menacing prod of Mr Coon's Winchester. 'Let's get this straight,' he went on, 'and fast, while we got the chance, 'cus right now there's a mean-tongued sheriff with an appetite for hangings and a

30

whole posse of like-minded deputies not two miles back headin' right this way, so if we don't — '

'You been tanglin' with the law?' snapped Mr Coon. 'Boys ain't goin' to like that, not one bit they ain't.'

'To hell with the boys!' flared McGinley, stepping forward, one eye on the Winchester. 'Yuh ain't never goin' to see yuh boys again if we don't shift! Now, yuh either step aside and let me ride on — you ain't on the sheriff's hangin' list, but yuh sure as hell will be if you're caught along of me — or we all three of us get movin' to some place way out of sight and reach. Choice is yours.' McGinley relaxed his weight to one hip. 'Or yuh could, of course, shoot me where I stand.'

'Johnstown,' said Wilbur. 'We head fast for Johnstown. Stay with the original plan. Deliver Boyd here to the boys. You agree, Mr Coon?'

'I agree. Fake and Mart will know what to do.'

'Right, so we ride, mister,' smiled

Wilbur. 'Take the track south. And no messin' now. We got your word on it?'

'Yuh got my word on it,' sighed McGinley despairingly. 'Anything, just so long as we don't waste no more time.'

Mr Coon gestured for McGinley to mount up. 'Lucky we found yuh when we did, eh?' he grinned. 'Might've gotten yourself killed otherwise.'

Impossible, thought McGinley on another sigh. Frank Boyd had died days back in a remote mountain cabin. What would the Johnstown 'boys' have to say about that when they discovered McGinley's true identity?

If, of course, they did.

5

The track south was slow, hard going through an increasingly thickening snowfall on a plummeting temperature that seemed to McGinley to grip and freeze every inch of exposed skin. But if it was tough and slow progress for the three men heading for Johnstown, it would be equally rough for the sheriff and his posse. So much so, McGinley hoped, that their fervour and frenzy for a hanging had been replaced by the more basic needs of warmth, shelter and a dry bed. Even a lynch mob felt the cold.

Thus, on the more hopeful possibility of the posse having turned for home, McGinley had come to the pressing problems of the dead man in the cabin — and who had shot him — Mr Coon and Wilbur, Johnstown, the waiting group of 'boys' and the unknown future awaiting the man mistakenly identified as Frank Boyd.

The thoughts had chilled and raised an icy sweat across his back. It was obvious that Mr Coon and Wilbur had never met Frank Boyd, but somebody had known him well enough to pass on a description of his prized Winchester and the clothes he would be wearing. Who, wondered McGinley, might that have been? The man who had shot him? But why, and did that mean the Johnstown 'boys' had similarly never met Boyd? But who was Frank Boyd and why was he wanted in Johnstown? And why had he been shot?

A whole sight more to the point, how long before it was revealed that McGinley was not Boyd, and what then?

Mr Coon and Wilbur had offered nothing further by way of explanation of themselves, Johnstown, or the waiting 'boys' as they negotiated the painfully treacherous track south. Who could blame them? Talk had no priority in the struggle against the wild terrain and foul weather. And even the strain of thought weakened in the effort.

The best McGinley could promise himself was to beat a hasty retreat out of Johnstown at the first chance to come his way. Which, when he reckoned it, had become something of a pattern of late.

However, still no sight or sounds of the sheriff and his men. Maybe he was getting lucky, he mused — whoever *he* was, had become or was going to be.

If he lived long enough to find out.

★　★　★

Johnstown wore the description 'town' on a threadbare sleeve. It had been founded haphazardly on the shifting fortunes of mining and miners, through times of boom when somebody struck it rich, to months of despair when nobody had a deal more than the clothes they stood in, the prized pick and shovel, and a heart, if not always a head, full of hope.

Its very shape mirrored its mixed fortunes. There was a street, or a swamp of mud and dirt that passed for one, around which had been ranged a collection of ramshackle timber buildings — a saloon, a mercantile, a livery — with most of the living dwellings consisting of what could be devised from spare planks, discarded crates and spreads of canvas.

Viewed from almost any angle from any approach in any weather, Johnstown was a heap without shape or proper structure. But no one much cared or had the inclination for change.

The real business of the town lay along the banks of the creek streams that gushed from the mountain ranges. It was here, and in the rock faces, plateaux and reaches of the cruel Colorado peaks, that men bent their backs, gave their every breath and sometimes their lives in the quest for gold and silver. It was in the daily routines of panning, digging, sifting and searching that Johnstown's fate and future lay.

But one man had more say in that fate than most.

Moses Barton had mined for the 'riches of God's good, wholesome earth' since being old enough and strong enough to lift a shovel. Legend and the romance of it told of him having made a half-a-dozen fortunes and lost them in the next big gamble that would open up the 'seam of a lifetime'. He was currently into his seventh fortune and still only in his mid-fifties.

If the sprawling mess and unwholesome smells of Johnstown could be laid at anyone's feet, Moses Barton was the man. It was he who had 'discovered' the potential of the area, completed the early surveys of it, mined it, exploited it and now controlled it. If you wanted to pan for gold, or mine for silver anywhere within a twenty-mile radius of Johnstown, you did so courtesy of Moses Barton, paid your rents due to him on time, never complained and delivered the agreed percentage share of any good fortune without qualm or query.

Between times you availed yourself of the liquor and girls at Barton's saloon, arranged for the credit for your victuals at Barton's mercantile, and, if you were still wealthy enough to own a horse, stabled it at Barton's livery.

'Only here to serve and look to your health and well-being,' was Moses' concluding promise to the new arrivals intent on digging for a fortune.

To which, some said, he might have added, 'and shoot yuh if yuh get out of line!' And maybe he, or one of his henchmen, would too, seeing as how Moses Barton was also the law, the only law, in Johnstown.

★ ★ ★

It was to this shapeless, soulless sprawl deep in the grip of the Colorado winter that Mr Coon and Wilbur led McGinley as the last of that bleak day's light faded on a still scattering snowfall and the wind snarled round them like a bad-tempered dog.

They stabled their mounts and slid away through the frozen mud, snow and ice to a tumbledown wooden shack in the darkness beyond the fitfully lit main street.

'If a fella name of Moses Barton crosses yuh path, yuh stay polite and keep your mouth shut. He's big time round here. Owns the place and we don't meddle,' Mr Coon had warned as he reached the shack, knocked, waited for the grunted response and opened the door on a wafting rush of liquor and tobacco-laced air.

McGinley had coughed, blinked, shuffled forward uncomfortably and been a full half minute before adjusting his sight to the pale, muted glow of the lantern light and the shapes in the thick, smoke-streaked shadows.

'Welcome,' said a gruff, wheezing voice from a corner. 'Fake Morgan. You must be Boyd. And about time too.'

'Ain't no cause for rancour there,' croaked another, easier going voice from the far side of the room beyond the cluttered table and rickety chairs. 'Name's Mart Peters. That's Benny Squires back of yuh. Mr Coon and Wilbur yuh already met. Glad to meet yuh, Frank.'

'Yeah, well,' began McGinley, 'there's somethin' yuh should know — '

Wilbur's tongue clicked anxiously. 'Some fella we got here, Mart,' he grinned on a croaky giggle. 'Keeps insistin' he ain't Frank Boyd. 'Course, we know different. There's the clothes and his Winchester's somethin' else. Take a look.' Wilbur passed the rifle through the shadows to a waiting hand. 'Travellin' incog . . . incog . . . '

'Incognito,' aided Mr Coon.

'Yeah, that,' clicked Wilbur. 'But we got to him, sure enough. And then shifted smartish too, eh, Mr Coon?'

'Frank says there's a sheriff trackin' him,' said Mr Coon, relaxing his weight

40

against the door.

'The law?' snapped Morgan. 'F'Cris'sake, that's the last thing we want in a situation like this. We get to attractin' the law around us — '

'Ease up there,' soothed Mart Peters, coughing lightly. 'Fella the likes of Frank Boyd is always bein' tracked. Lead-spittin' sheriffs go with the territory, ain't that so, Frank?'

McGinley had opened his mouth to begin his long explanation of himself and his circumstances, when Wilbur had clicked again and hurried into another giggled outburst.

'Anyhow,' he grinned, 'we didn't waste no time. Came down on the fast South track. And we didn't see nobody. Nothin'. Not so much as a hare. Ain't that so, Mr Coon?'

'That's just so, Wilbur.'

'Good,' said Peters, before McGinley could make another attempt at explanation 'then we ain't got no problems. Leastways, none that Frank here can't handle. So mebbe we could

41

get to the plannin', eh? Talk it through. What yuh reckon, Frank? How yuh figurin' on liftin' fifty thousand in gold? It's what we hired yuh for, so you tell us, eh?'

6

When the rattler stares, you do not blink, had been a maxim McGinley had learned and followed early in his wanderlust lifestyle. And this, he decided quickly, gulping on the thickening air of the shack, was a situation that called for doing just that: no blinking; see this one out as best he could, and trust to luck.

He was in a rattler's nest and the occupant was staring.

'Yuh thought this through full circle?' clipped Morgan.

'Takes time and plannin' for what yuh got in mind,' croaked McGinley as convincingly as his dry, cracked voice would permit.

'See,' said Peters, slapping his hands together, 'what did I tell yuh? Said as how Frank Boyd was a man for plannin', didn't I? Didn't I say just that?'

'Just that, Mart,' clicked Wilbur.

'Your very words,' echoed Mr Coon.

'That's how yuh pulled the Silver Springs' job, weren't it, Frank?' continued Peters. 'Timin', plannin'. That so, Frank?'

'Well — ' began McGinley, shifting uncomfortably.

''Course,' enthused Peters, hurrying on, 'the Springs weren't nothin' alongside the raid at North Forks. Now that *was* a raid. Tell 'em how yuh pulled that, Frank. Go on, tell 'em.'

McGinley gulped again. 'Weren't easy,' he began. 'None of 'em ever are — not if yuh want a neat, clean job.' He paused, conscious of the shadows filling with concentrated stares. 'Yuh gotta pick your time and place,' he floundered, daring to blink. 'And yuh men. You sure as hell gotta pick yuh men.'

'Now there,' interrupted Peters, 'we do have an edge. Yuh reckon that, Fake?'

'Some,' said Morgan, his stare tight on McGinley's face.

44

Peters slapped his hands again. 'Sure we have. Take Benny here. Benny's out of Wisconsin. Rode with Clam Butler and his boys. In on the railroad hold-up at One Rock. Remember that? And then there's Mr Coon and Wilbur. They been around some, ain't yuh, fellas? Down South. The Eastman Bank job. Brownsville . . . the Riversdale raid.' He grinned broadly. 'We got some real experience here, eh? And that's not to mention Fake. Speak up for yourself, Fake.'

Morgan leaned forward from the gloom so that his stare seemed to come alight. 'Frank'd know all about me, wouldn't yuh, Frank?'

McGinley twitched but steadied his nerve and his gaze. 'Sure I would,' he smiled. 'Who wouldn't?' He let the smile fade slowly.

'And then there's y'self, Mart,' added Benny Squires, flicking his fingers over the butt of his holstered Colt. 'Frank's sure to have heard of you. Ain't nobody *not* heard of that day in Richmond.

There m'self and I saw it all, so I *know*.'

'Yeah, well,' said Peters, 'that was eighteen months back and Frank could've been some place else. That so, Frank?'

'You know me, always on the move,' grinned McGinley, beginning to sweat. 'Let's see now,' he mused, 'eighteen months back . . . that'd be Falls Junction.' He paused, uncertain of where to head in his fictional wandering.

'Falls Junction?' frowned Mr Coon. 'Why that'd be the shootin' of Chems Parton. You in on that, Frank?'

McGinley had stiffened at the mention of the name and the suddenly flooding images of the saloon bar at Remarkable. 'Chems ain't dead,' he said carefully. 'He didn't die in Falls Junction.'

'That's right,' said Fake Morgan, coming to his feet. 'Chems Parton ain't dead. He rode clear of the Falls. Last seen around this territory. You crossed him, Frank?'

'No,' lied McGinley, 'can't say I have. But, then, I been holed-up some.'

'At the cabin,' quipped Peters. 'No place for a fella like yourself, eh, Frank? Cooped up, all that weather closin' in. T'ain't natural. And yuh look worn with it. Could do with a decent night's sleep, eh? Well, we can fix that easy enough. Another room back of this one. Benny, you give up your bed for Frank here. Right? Good. Help yourself to what we got here, Frank — food, whiskey, coupla gals when yuh fancy — and we'll get to the talkin' and plannin' at first light, eh, when you're feelin' fresher? That suit yuh?'

That would suit very well; very well indeed, thought McGinley, nodding to Peters as he followed Benny Squires to the back room.

He blinked on the new, deeper gloom, but there were no rattlers here. For the moment.

★   ★   ★

McGinley had not the slightest intention of sleeping or coming within a nod of it. He was way out of his depth here, he had decided, and not only floundering but fast heading for a drowning.

He could not even begin to imagine what wild scheme for the robbery of $50,000 in gold Mart Peters and Fake Morgan had dreamed up, save that the gold must be here in Johnstown and Mart and Fake knew exactly where. Nor could he imagine how it was that Frank Boyd had been 'hired' into the planning; nor did he know who in hell Frank Boyd had been. But he did know that he was certainly very dead, shot close up by . . . who *had* pulled the trigger on Frank, and where was he now?

It was also chillingly obvious that it was only a matter of time before McGinley's true identity was revealed. He had the prickly sensation in the nape of his neck that Fake Morgan already had his suspicions. The cold light of day might confirm the worst.

'So,' McGinley had sighed and frowned, 'what now?' He still had his warm clothes and he might get lucky and slip his mount clear of the livery without too much fuss, but he had lost the Winchester into Mart Peters' care. That might prove a disadvantage for what he had in mind, but he would have to take his chances as they came if he was going to be clear of Johnstown by dawn.

And he was — that or die in the attempt.

He crossed to the window of the bunk-room, tested that it opened without too much noise and peered through it for what he could see of Johnstown by night.

Little enough: the dark sprawl of the main street, shapes of broken buildings, tents, the flotsam of mining, snow piled in brooding heaps, the occasional light at the window of a poor sleeper, or some unfortunate whore's place of business; the livery dark and silent; a larger, more imposing shack on higher ground at the northern end of the town, a light in one window — and the shape of a man slipping low and hunched through the shadows towards it.

It was almost a full minute before McGinley realized the figure was Fake Morgan and that the man who opened the door of the shack to greet him was none other than Chems Parton.

7

It took just two more minutes for McGinley to reach a second firm conclusion: if Chems Parton and Fake Morgan were together in some conspiracy he could not begin to fathom, McGinley's assumed identity as Frank Boyd would be blown within seconds of Parton setting eyes on him. Another good reason for putting Johnstown way behind him, he figured. And now the sooner the better.

He waited an hour, until he thought the town to be deserted of even a stray hound and the residents deep in sleep, the main room of the shack all quiet save for the snoring of Mr Coon and the habitual clicking of Wilbur's tongue, and the snowfall little more than vague flakes on a light breeze.

Then he moved.

Climbing through the bunk-room

window, dropping silently to the frozen ground, closing the window behind him and slipping into the tightest shadows, proved easy enough. It was the next move that might be tricky, he reckoned.

He needed to reach the livery quickly and in one uninterrupted dash, no time for hesitation, moving too slowly, watching and waiting. Just one dash, no messing.

There was still a light in the window of the shack visited by Morgan, and for one brief moment McGinley was tempted to move closer to it if only to satisfy his curiosity and perhaps soothe his annoyance. Chems Parton had a heap of troubles to atone for where McGinley was concerned . . . But that apart, just what was Parton doing here in Johnstown; was he the owner of the imposing shack, or was he in somebody else's pay; and precisely what was at the root of the tie in with Fake Morgan? Fifty-thousand dollars in gold? Did Mart Peters and his boys know of Morgan's association?

McGinley decided he would be long gone from Johnstown before he had the answers.

He pulled the collar of his coat high into his neck, glanced quickly left to right, listened for a moment to the still snoring sleepers in the shack, and slid away.

He had reached the livery in only minutes, checked that the blacksmith was sleeping in his living quarters, and moved on tiptoe into the stabling area, when a horse snorted nervously and a shadow that seconds before had seemed to be one of a cluster broke free and slid across the floor towards him.

*   *   *

The barrel of the Colt, the gun firm and levelled in a steady grip, came ahead of the bulk of the man, a tall, heavily built figure with one eye hooded and dull, the other wet and gleaming and fixed like a beam on McGinley's face.

'Seen yuh before, ain't I?' hissed the man, halting at the edge of the faint patch of light. 'Stabled yuh mount here a while back.' He sniffed loudly. 'You checked in with Mr Barton yet?'

McGinley grunted, his gaze still on the Colt and the levelled barrel. 'Who's he?' he asked with a shrug of innocence. 'He the sheriff or somethin'?'

'Moses Barton is the law hereabouts, mister, and he don't take kindly to folk trespassin' all over his town as the fancy takes.'

'Trespassin'?' croaked McGinley. 'Hell, I ain't nothin' like no trespasser. Passin' through. Matter of fact, I'm leavin' right now. Soon as I got my horse saddled up and packed. No problem. No trespassin', I assure yuh.'

'Not as easy as that, fella,' mouthed the man, the hooded eye flickering. 'Yuh don't just ride in and out of Johnstown without Moses Barton knowin' to it. So yuh'll do as I say, right now. We'll go see what the big man has to say.'

There was to be no arguing with that Colt, thought McGinley, conscious of the prodding threat of the barrel. Barton's henchman was as used to pulling on the trigger as he was of whip-lashing the barrel at an obstinate head. And he had the muscle to go with it!

'Mite late for visitin', ain't it?' said McGinley backing carefully.

'No matter, Mr Barton ain't abed yet.'

'Light sleeper, eh? Know the feelin'.' McGinley glanced quickly to his left, to the deep shadows of an empty stall. 'Even so, wouldn't want to impose,' he shrugged. 'Mebbe we could leave this 'til mornin'.'

The man shuffled a step forward. 'Where you been all night, mister?' he asked, the wet eye brightening. 'Seen yuh with them two minin' fellas. Where's the tie-in with them? You a miner?'

'Miner?' scoffed McGinley. 'Hell, no. Wouldn't give yuh a spit for no pick

55

and pannin' graft. Me, I'm all for cattle. Big, open spaces. Prairie life. Herds of solid beef. Like I say, just passin' through. Headin' down Texas way.' He had drawn level with the empty stall and halted. 'Like to get started. Long ride.'

'Later,' growled the man, the gun arm stiffening. 'You'll see Mr Barton first. Right now.'

It was as the barrel of the Colt had prodded a fraction closer, that McGinley judged it to be within his grasp. His right hand flashed, settling on the piece like a vice, at the same time drawing the man towards him.

The henchman lost his balance in his surprise and the momentum of McGinley's heaving tug. He groaned, slid forward unaware of McGinley's knee already lifting and thrusting deep and painfully into his groin.

The man gasped, moaned, spat; his wet eye flooded, the hooded one closed. McGinley's knee thrust again, this time with his grip on the Colt wrenching it free of the man's hand.

Ten seconds later the barrel had been whipped viciously across the man's temple and he was bundled unconscious and bleeding into the empty stall where he lay like a punctured sack of feed meal, both eyes hooded.

McGinley murmured soothingly to the nervy mounts and waited until the livery lay in silence again and the winter's night tightened in the cold. Only then did he check the Colt — fully loaded — and ease it gratefully into his belt. He was beginning to feel like his old self.

Whoever that was supposed to be.

★　★　★

Again, he waited, watching from the shadows for the slightest movement, listening for the softest sound that could not be readily explained and identified. Nothing, save the snorts of the mounts as they settled, the clip of a hoof, scuff of straw bedding, his own

57

breathing and, not least, the beat of his heart.

Two minutes . . . three. The henchman stayed slumped and unconscious; the blacksmith, snug in a mound of blankets, slept on; Johnstown stiffened in the cold, frosted air; smoke curled from chimneys.

But there was still a light burning in the window of the shack. Were Parton and Fake Morgan still there, still talking? Was Moses Barton with them?

No time to waste finding out. He would take his chance of being spotted as he left town; head high into the snow-hugged mountains along tracks no sane fellow would follow, steering well clear of the route by which he had fled Remarkable — just in case the hanging sheriff had been bull-headed enough not to give up the hunt.

As for Mart Peters and his sidekicks, he guessed they would have to plot their own way round the problems of stealing $50,000 in gold.

McGinley had collected his saddle,

had the blanket on the back of his mount and was whispering reassuringly to the horse when he heard the steps crunching through the snow beyond the livery.

He patted the mount, removed the blanket and slid back to the deepest shadows, an icy sweat prickling in the nape of his neck as he waited for whoever it was approaching to reach the stables.

And praying quietly that the unconscious henchman in the empty stall would stay sleeping.

8

'Luke — what the hell yuh doin' back there?' The voice cracked across the darkness like splintering ice, the words hanging on the air as if frozen. 'Luke — yuh hearin' me there? Yuh been gone half the night, damnit. Yuh got some gal tucked away? Boss wants yuh.'

McGinley had a face to the voice long before Chems Parton had crossed from the snow to the far end of the livery where he stood, frowning, peering into the inky interior for a sight of the henchman, Luke.

'Luke,' he called again, this time with a hissed urgency, 'yuh hear what I said, the boss is wantin' yuh. Shouldn't keep him waitin' at this hour of the day. Yuh know how he can be.'

McGinley stiffened, his fingers soft on the butt of the Colt, gaze unblinking as he waited for Parton to move. How long before he slid along the line of stalls? Would Luke stay unconscious, or would the sound of Parton's voice make him stir?

'I ain't for messin' with,' grumbled Parton, stamping his feet agaist the cold, blowing warm breath across his fingers. 'Not in this weather I ain't. And I got a cosy bed waitin' on me back there. Now, just where in hell are yuh?'

The man came slowly, carefully along the line, squinting intently into each stall, patting the flanks of the mounts, murmuring quietly to them, scuffing his boots through the bedding.

'Luke, in God's name what yuh — '

The moan rose from the shadows as if turned on the wind. Parton froze where he stood. McGinley tensed, the Colt drawn and firm in his hand.

'Luke?' hissed the man again, sidling stealthily towards the stall where the henchman was already stirring. 'How come . . . ? What in tarnation — ?'

McGinley stepped from the depths of the darkness with the gun barrel raised for the whip that would fall across the back of Parton's head. He grunted with the effort, eased aside as the body slumped, then stepped over it and settled another blow on the henchman's head.

'And just stay right there, f'Cris'sake!' he croaked, slipping the Colt to his belt again as he turned his attention to his mount. 'Saddle up and ride,' he murmured to himself, smoothing the blanket across the horse's back.

His luck had held this far, but he was asking a lot to suppose he could push it much further. It only needed . . . Hell, more crunching steps. Another body on the move. Who this time? The blacksmith, Fake Morgan, one of Peters' men? Did it matter? There were no friendly faces in Johnstown.

He finished the saddling up, checked the girth, whispered to the mount and led it gently from the stall. Two minutes, that was all it was going to take to lead the horse from the livery to the snow, mount up and ride out. He would be one of the shadows in three.

The man appeared silhouetted at the entrance to the stables as if he had risen like a phantom.

'Goin' some place, mister?' growled Benny Squires, straddling the space, a rifle clutched tight across him. 'Don't reckon on the boys appreciatin' that.'

Nothing for it now, decided McGinley. Mount up right here and ride like the whip of a plains' wind!

★ ★ ★

He was mounted and bringing the horse round, taking in the loose rein to a firm grip in one hand, drawing the Colt from his belt again with the other, when Chems Parton clawed back to his feet, staggered and thudded against the side of the stall.

'You, damn yuh!' he groaned, his eyes squinting for a focused gaze on McGinley. 'The fella in the bar . . . Remarkable. Sonofabitch! How the hell did yuh — ?'

McGinley's Colt blazed as his mount rose on its hindlegs, pawed air for a moment, clattered to all-fours again and came to its stride under the flick of the reins.

He gave the sprawled, bleeding body of Parton no more than a sidelong glance, whooped the horse into action, slung himself low to its neck and rode hell-for-leather for the entrance where Benny Squires waited, his rifle already probing into an aim.

'Yuh ain't goin' no place, mister,' bellowed Squires, standing tight and firm, legs still straddled. 'Hold it up there, right now. Yuh hearin' me?'

McGinley's only concentration was on bringing the gunslinger into range of his Colt as the mount raced on, nostrils flared, eyes like wild moons, its every muscle heaving under the tension of the pace.

Behind him now, caught in the noise, the drift of lingering gunsmoke, the smells of blood and sweat, the stabled mounts were beginning to panic, tugging at the loose ropes tethering them.

The dazed henchman, Luke, had heaved himself upright, rolled drunkenly from the empty stall to one occupied by a nerve-fazed bucking horse only to be felled by a vicious hindleg kick.

He lay still again, this time bleeding at the temple.

McGinley waited until the very last second of his charge for the night before releasing the venom of the Colt. Squires had remained straddled, uncertain of his target, almost mesmerized by the charging horse, so that he saw nothing of McGinley's drawn gun low across the animal's neck.

And when he did move, finally flinging himself to his left, it was to fall directly into McGinley's line of fire.

The Colt roared and spat.

Squires grimaced, lost his grip on the rifle, fell back and was as still as the frozen snow when McGinley's mount cleared his body in one leap and was into the darkness and lost before he had twitched his last.

The shots, the panicking horses, the shouts and moans had brought Johnstown to a sudden, bleary-eyed life, a blaze of lights flickering at windows, silhouetting the shapes behind canvas.

Men called across the darkness to each other, firing questions faster than they could struggle into pants and hitch braces. Bar girls were tipped unceremoniously from warm beds as fellows reached for clothes and checked over their Colts. Even the few town drunks opened their eyes and figured for it being a dark start to the day.

Only two men in Johnstown that night stood with their gazes set deep into the darkness beyond the shacks and jumbled shapes to where the snow-topped peaks of the high mountains gleamed like white breasts.

One was Moses Barton, the other Mart Peters. And both, had they known it, had the same thing firmly in mind.

Retribution.

9

He looked what he had become, a man hacked crudely out of the rock, no soft heart here, no smooth edges; nobody ever pushed Moses Barton aside. They went round him.

'He got Chems and Luke. Sonofabitch!' he growled, his back to the fire, eyes gleaming through the lantern-lit glow to the shadows at the back of the shack. 'He'll pay for that. Pay hard and long as I can drag it out. Set yuh marks to it, yuh hear?'

The two men facing him, Clem Dragge and 'Pieces' Cooper, grunted their understanding, nodded and shifted their feet uncomfortably.

'Bad night,' murmured Dragge. 'Chems, Luke, that fella Squires . . . And we ain't got a clue as to who the killer is.'

'S'right,' agreed Cooper. 'Sorta just rode in.'

'Nobody *sorta just rides in*,' snapped Barton. 'Somebody brought him here. And for a purpose. He weren't no miner, that's for sure. Never has been.'

'Fake Morgan was here earlier,' said Dragge carefully.

'What yuh sayin'?' frowned Barton.

'Fella might just be tied in with him. Another gun in the bunch.'

'Who then shoots up one of the bunch? Don't seem likely.'

Cooper shifted again. 'What's Fake Morgan and them boys ridin' along of him doin' here, anyhow?' he asked.

'Mebbe Chems had found out,' said Dragge.

Barton sighed and thrust his hands to a locked grip behind him. 'I'll tell yuh what the likes of Fake Morgan is doin' here,' he scowled, his gaze burning over the men. 'He's here for the same reason as every other dirtpickin' fella: gold. Only he, I figure, ain't much for diggin' and pannin' for it.'

'He's plannin' on stealin' it?' said Dragge.

'Hell,' coughed Cooper.

'I figure so.' Barton's stare deepened. 'There's fifty thousand of mining fellas' gold in its raw state up there in the main shaft simply waitin' on the weather to ease to shift it. Common knowledge hereabouts. T'ain't no secret. There for anybody to see if they care to climb to it.'

'Mebbe so,' spluttered Dragge, 'but that ain't sayin' anybody's got the means to stealin' it. Not up there, not in the mountains; not this weather.'

Barton's grin slid like a loose scar to the corner of his mouth. 'Don't learn much, do yuh, Clem? Don't keep yuh eyes open, do yuh? Ain't yuh learned yet that where gold's concerned there's always a way, always the means, and it don't matter how many die for it? High mountains, bad weather, no trail; cold, snow, wind, ice . . . Bah! Man dazzled blind by the prospect of gold — 'specially fifty thousand dollars' worth of it — sees only gold. There ain't nothin' else.'

'So yuh reckonin' on Fake and them other fleas-cratchin' types bein' here to help themeselves?' said Cooper.

'Ain't in a place like Johnstown this time of year for their health and the scenery, are they?' Barton's hands broke from the grip behind him and settled in his pockets. 'They're here to lift gold. Seen hundreds just like 'em.'

'So where's that leave us?' asked Dragge. 'What's yuh thinkin', Mr Barton?'

'Plain enough. We provision up at first light and head after that scumbag who shot Chems and did for Luke. I want to reckon with him.' Barton's grin cracked loose again. 'And when we done with that, we'll go take a look at that fifty thousand, eh? Just check it's still safe — and make very certain there ain't no meddlin' hands gettin' itchy round it. Ain't arguin' with that, are yuh?'

Neither man said a word.

★ ★ ★

70

Wilbur clicked his tongue nervously. Mr Coon hummed tunelessly. Fake Morgan played idly with an empty Colt.

'He ain't Frank Boyd, is he? We got it wrong.' Mart Peters emptied the dregs of a whiskey bottle to a tin mug, gulped it in one and gazed over the faces of the men gathered in the shadow-stifled shack. 'Right, ain't I? I ain't misunderstandin' what Fake here found out.'

'That's so, Mart,' murmured Mr Coon. 'I ain't disputin' one word of what Fake's told us as to how Chems Parton shot Boyd when he'd left Remarkable and was hell-leatherin' it from a crazed-sheriff. Ain't arguin' that one bit.'

'I just knew it. Knew it,' grunted Morgan as if talking to himself. 'Minute I set eyes on the fella. If that's Frank Boyd, I said, I'm a Chinaman. Didn't have the look, the stare. Sure, he had Boyd's clothes, and his gun, but he weren't Frank Boyd, not no how. So I put it straight to Parton, and he told me the story . . . And now, damn it, we lost Benny.'

'We could mebbe put that to rights, eh?' said Wilbur. 'Go get the sonofabitch, whoever he is, wherever he is.'

'We could do that, sure enough,' agreed Mr Coon. 'Owe that much to Benny.'

Wilbur clicked his tongue in a sudden flurry of anger and nerves. 'Hell, ain't that fella one helluva snake? Took out Benny, Chems Parton, that other sidekick . . . What sorta devil is he, f'Cris'sake? Tell yuh somethin' else, that old rattler, Moses Barton, ain't goin' to be one bit pleased about Chems. Heard it said as how he treated him like his own.'

'Heard that, too,' echoed Mr Coon.

'Shame you two weren't a sight smarter in rumblin' that the fella weren't Boyd,' grumbled Morgan.

Wilbur's mouth erupted in a shower of clicked saliva. 'Now you hold right on there, Fake Morgan. Mr Coon and me did the best we could under the circumstances, and we weren't in no way — '

'All right, hold it!' flared Mart Peters, banging the tin mug on the table. 'Ain't nothin' to be had in goin' round and round what's over and done with. Chems and Benny are dead, so's the sidekick, and the man we thought was Boyd killed 'em and happens, right now, to be ridin' free. Ain't *that* just somethin' to be real proud of?' he sneered.

'No,' said Mr Coon. 'It ain't, but on the other hand — '

'On the other hand,' snapped Peters, 'we ain't one spit closer to what we trailed into this godforsaken dump for in the first place.'

'Gold,' murmured Mr Coon.

'Precisely,' glowered Peters. 'So let's get back to that, shall we — without the benefit of Mr Frank Boyd's expert knowledge on how to lift, transport and get away with fifty thousand dollars' of the stuff.'

'Well,' clicked Wilbur, at the same

time blowing at the brim of his hat, 'we know where it is.' He grinned. 'Up there, in them mountains.' The grin faded. 'In *this* weather.'

'And we also know *where* in them mountains in this weather, don't we?' added Mr Coon with a knowing nod. 'Stacked neat as a pin in the entrance tunnel to the main shaft.'

'And here's somethin' else we know,' clipped Morgan. 'Yuh can take it sure as night to sun-up that Moses Barton is saddlin' up right now, coupla gunslingers along of him, all set to trek high into them same mountains. And for why? To gun down the man who shot Chems Parton.'

'Now, if that's the case — ' began Wilbur.

'Don't get ahead of y'self, Wilbur,' grinned Peters. 'Fake and me see what's coming. You figure that if Barton is goin' to be so fully occupied trackin' down the so-called Frank Boyd, we ain't goin' to have no trouble in getting ourselves, uninterruped, into that main shaft. That it?'

74

'Took the words from my mouth, Mart. Words from my mouth. We could do it too,' enthused Mr Coon. 'Might get lucky with the weather, ain't goin' to be more than a handful of men guardin' the gold; four of us . . . Yep, we could do it.'

'And Benny Squires?' leered Morgan. 'What about him? Yuh were all for settlin' his account minute or so back.'

'Benny would understand,' said Wilbur.

'Sure he would,' followed Mr Coon.

'Well, one thing's for certain, yuh ain't for askin' him, are yuh?' leered Morgan again.

Mart Peters eased back in his chair at the table and stared deep into the shadows. 'Amazin', ain't it,' he said quietly, 'what men will do when the word *gold* escapes somebody's lips? Amazin' . . . ' His stare hardened. 'Well, that may be so, but when we pull outa here, we're doin' it as much for Benny as ourselves, and don't nobody forget it. And somethin' else yuh'd best not forget, we get so much as a flicker of a sight of that sonofabitch who did for our good friend, we go get him. No messin'. Any man who don't, answers to me.'

Wilbur clicked his tongue anxiously. Mr Coon hummed sonorously. Fake Morgan spun the empty chamber of the Colt for the last time.

And the shadows crept closer and began to breathe.

10

The only track passable out of Johnstown on that night of the shooting at the livery had been the mine trail heading north, high into the mountains to where, for close on thirty years, men had lived and died in the search for gold.

McGinley had taken it in a simple bid to stay breathing. The snowfall had been scattered, the wind was easy but ice-cold, and the light fitful from an uncertain night sky. The going, what there was of it on the packed snow trail, had been slow and uncertain, with the mount picking at each footfall and McGinley having little choice but to let it. If it was slow for him, he reasoned, it would be no easier for anybody caring to follow.

But who would bother, he wondered? In spite of losing Benny Squires, surely Mart Peters and Morgan would call it a day, realizing their bad mistake in confusing McGinley for Frank Boyd, and get back to sorting the problems of gold — all fifty thousand of them. Or would they seek revenge?

Revenge might well be uppermost in the mind of Moses Barton. The henchman, Luke, he would replace as if making a purchase at some two-bit saloon. Always more when the bottle was empty . . .

The loss of Chems Parton could be a whole lot different. How close had Moses and Parton been; what had they shared; what had been Parton's worth? You could bet your life the gunslinging scumbag's value would be measured by gold standards.

Only problem for McGinley in Parton's death out here, was that the hanging-happy sheriff of Remarkable would never get to hear Chem's confession to the shooting of Hank Green. Shame.

McGinley had ridden on, climbing ever higher into the bleak winter mountains, the snowfall beginning to swirl on a strengthening wind from the east. Another hour at most, he reckoned, and he would be forced to seek shelter, rest the mount and himself until first light.

And not least take stock of just where he was, what he had and where he was heading.

He tapped the butt of his Colt tight in his belt. Half empty. He grunted. Going to have to do something about that if he was ever going to clear this country in anything like a breathing piece.

* * *

The hour passed and brought McGinley to a higher sprawl of rocks and boulders and the welcoming shelter of an overhang.

He reined the mount to a halt, slid from the saddle to the frozen ground, unpacked his bedroll and flung it across his shoulders. Minutes later, he was huddled close to the horse for extra warmth, a cheroot finally lit and soothing as he contemplated the likely source of the glow he was certain he had seen in the higher reaches.

He was deep into mining country now, an area normally alive with the sounds of men at work, hacking, digging, shovelling, panning the creek streams on the lower slopes, ripping at the very guts of the mountains for the sudden gleam that would announce gold — thousands of dollars' worth of it for some; a dream into nowhere for most.

But men and mining carried their own baggage, even in the depths of winter; cabins, shacks, some fellows left to stand guard over claims and equipment, some preferring to do so, others sitting it out in caves to await the first thaw and the sun climbing higher.

There were others here, somewhere, he thought. Question was, did he try to make contact, or did he keep moving, silently and alone?

Had the glow he had seen been a fire, lantern light? If he tried reaching it at sun-up would he be welcome, or shot on sight?

And just how long was it going to take Moses Barton to unleash his venom?

He grunted, drew on the cheroot until the tip came alive and watched the smoke curl crazily on the whipping wind. Sooner or later he was going to need food for himself and his mount; probably sooner, along with warmth, if the weather did not break.

He grunted again and patted the horse. Chances of clearing the mountains unnoticed, unseen, alone, even in the depths of winter, were remote, he reckoned. So . . . 'We move first hint of light,' he murmured. 'And to hell with it!'

The mount flicked its ears and snorted.

'Yeah, me too!' grinned McGinley behind another curl of smoke.

* * *

The snowfall had eased again and the first break of light through the eastern skies promised a later brightness when McGinley packed the bedroll, mounted up and reined the horse back to the vague outline of trail.

The going again was slow and sometimes treacherous as the mount picked and poked its way north. The rocky sweeps to the peaks grew steeper, the giant boulder outcrops more bruised and bulging, and the sudden shelvings to cavernous creeks and deep-cut gulches more difficult to detect ahead of coming to the brink of them.

But the light grew stronger, brighter, as if determined to leave its mark, and after close on an hour of slipping and sliding ever northwards, McGinley began to feel that he might — *might*, given that touch of extra luck — make some valuable miles come noon and then another nightfall. What the hell, he mused, he might even —

And it was there, as the mount

picked its way clear of a sweep of ice-faced rock and approached the drop to a snow-packed creek, that McGinley's luck held its breath and he reined the horse tight at the crack and whine of a single rifle shot.

* * *

He sat tight, the mount short-reined to both hands, his knees gripping to steady the horse's instinctive reaction to buck and move on, and peered across the seemingly unbroken whiteness.

The light was strengthening fast now, lifting the shadows, smoothing a soft sheen and sparkle across the frost and snow — but revealing nothing at a first scan of the gleam of a rifle barrel.

McGinley murmured quietly to the mount, tightened the reins, narrowed his gaze and peered again, this time following and probing every lift and line of the creek. Was the gunman just sitting out there somewhere, he wondered, tucked among boulders, deep in a rock cleft, with McGinley in his sights, just waiting, watching? If he was going to fire again, get to it! But who was he, some isolated miner, one of Barton's henchmen, what was he doing out here? Where was he, damn it, and was he alone?

Maybe he should call out. One thing he dared not do was ride on, or draw his Colt. A wrong move now and he would be frozen dead meat in an hour.

His gaze roved on; a beading of sweat broke across his top lip; the horse flicked its ears, snorted, the breath rolling like steam on the thin morning air. Nothing down there in the creek, he thought, grunting softly, not so much as a shadow out of place, not even where they were at their thickest at the far end of the drift . . . And then he had it.

A bulk that was far from natural; deep in snow, but, damn it, it had a window, or two panes of glass that were showing. And now, as he concentrated his gaze, he could make out the slope of a roof, the hint of a chimney stack. A miner's shack, small and almost lost in the snowfall, but a shack, no denying that. And it had to be there, he reckoned, that the gunman was holed up, the rifle trained on him like a deadly finger.

No point in just sitting here, he figured, as the mount shifted impatiently. The cold was beginning to bite and time to press. So, there seemed nothing else for it . . .

'I'm comin' down,' he called, the sound of his voice echoing across the creek. 'If you're goin' to shoot, yuh'd best get to it, but I ain't spoilin' for no fight.'

And then he relaxed the reins and urged the mount forward.

The horse picked its way carefully under McGinley's encouragement and loose rein, its hoofs clicking, slipping across rock where they found it beneath the snow, seeking for a firmer hold where they fell into shale and frozen dirt. Step by step, click by click, slither by slither, but the distance was closing.

And thankfully, thought McGinley, the morning stayed silent. No more shots, but you could bet your life the gunman was still watching, still had his aim held steady, watching every step, judging every yard, waiting for the moment when a hand would drop from the reins and the fingers spread to the butt of a Colt. That would be the moment — the last for McGinley if he chose it.

He had come to within a few yards of the bulk and could see the window panes clearly — but no sight of a barrel, much less the blur of a face when he noted to his left the frame of a door almost covered with snow.

How long since it had opened, he wondered; how long since it had been closed and bolted against the Winter? Who the devil was behind it?

'Like I said, I ain't spoilin' for no fight,' he called again, his narrowed gaze shifting quickly from window to door, 'but if yuh plannin' on brewin' up some hot coffee there, sure would be a treat against this cold. Better still, yuh happen to have a bottle — '

He tensed at the grating slide of a bolt, the cracking of frost and ice as the door was prised open, at first slowly, then with a flourish and a lunging probe of the rifle barrel.

'Inside, and quick about it!' snapped the order from the dark interior of the shack.

McGinley gulped. No, he had not been mistaken: it had been a woman's voice snapping out the order.

11

There was almost a full minute of silence, total and complete without so much as the sound of breathing, before McGinley dared to shuffle a step forward from the door closed tight at his back.

'Hold it right there,' snapped the voice again. 'Yuh move when I say so. Ease that Colt to the table there front of you.'

'Anythin' you say,' shrugged McGinley. 'But like I told yuh, ma'am — '

'I know, I heard yuh the first time — yuh ain't for fightin'. That's as mebbe.'

McGinley slid the Colt to the table and peered for a shape and face to the voice. He made a pretence of shivering and rubbing his hands together for warmth. 'Do with a fire in here, ma'am, don't mind me sayin' so. Cold enough to crack yuh bones back there on the trail. Yuh want for me to light one?'

'There ain't no fuel and there ain't the time,' clipped the woman from the shadowed corner of the shack.

'Yuh goin' some place?' asked McGinley lightly, his gaze still probing for a face.

'We're goin' some place. You and me and that horse of yours.'

'That a fact, ma'am? Well, now, that depends on a whole heap of circumstances. I mean, I hadn't been plannin' exactly on — '

'I'm callin' the shots here, mister, and don't go thinkin' other.'

'So it seems,' said McGinley, moving carefully now to the side of the table, a foot closer to the shadowed corner. 'Well, that bein' the case, and seein' as how yuh got this notion of us gettin' t'gether — '

'Never said that.'

'Beggin' yuh pardon, ma'am. Anyhow, whatever, mebbe we should get to some sort of introductions, eh? How about that?' McGinley paused, his gaze settling on the gleam of the rifle barrel. 'Name's McGinley. Just that. Most folk just know me as McGinley. And yourself?'

Silence for long, empty seconds. 'Branham,' said the woman carefully. 'Charlotte Branham. Generally known as Charley — with a 'y'.'

McGinley grunted. 'Pretty name,' he smiled. 'Well, now, Charley with a 'y', what in tarnation is a girl with a name like that doin' out here in the middle of a Colorado winter? Don't mind me sayin' so, ma'am, but t'ain't exactly yuh everyday occurrence, is it?'

'Might ask the same of yourself,' said the woman. 'Can see yuh ain't no miner. I know 'em all hereabouts, and I ain't seen you before. Ain't heard the name neither. So what you doin' out here, mister?'

McGinley shuffled his feet. 'That, as they say, ma'am, is a long story and I ain't — '

'Yuh on the run?' quipped the woman. 'Yuh got that look about yuh.'

'That obvious?' said McGinley. 'Well,

I guess yuh could put it that way — '

'Yuh crossed Moses Barton. Yuh out of Johnstown?'

'I been there.' McGinley hesitated a moment, his gaze still on the rifle barrel, his mind spinning with the possibilities of grabbing it one-handed and yanking it clear of the woman's grip. 'Matter of fact,' he went on slowly, 'I shot Chems Parton last night, so I guess yuh might say — '

'Yuh did *what?*' said the woman lowering the barrel from its direct aim.

'Shot Chems Parton.'

'You're a dead man, mister! Moses Barton'll see yuh in Hell!'

McGinley shrugged and took another step forward. 'Sure,' he grinned, 'but he's gotta catch me first. And there's some queue linin' up ahead of him, I fancy. Yuh care to step out of them shadows, Charley with a 'y', and I'll be happy to tell yuh while I still got the breath . . . '

★ ★ ★

She was somewhere in her mid twenties, dark-haired, brown-eyed, with a full, sensual mouth and a figure, McGinley reckoned, that would turn a whole street of heads when not smothered in a mound of winter clothes topped by a long fur coat.

She had listened quietly, attentively, to McGinley's tale of events since his ill-fated ride into Remarkable. He had missed nothing, and concluded: 'So there yuh are — McGinley, or Frank Boyd if yuh prefer it, or just about anybody else yuh care to name, it seems! I leave it to you, ma'am. But yuh right, I'm on the run, clean out of these mountains if I can make it. And time, I regret to say, is fast desertin' me.' He had paused, traced a finger down the side of the scrubbed pine table, and been a full half-minute before speaking again. 'T'ain't none of my business, o'course, but if yuh'd care to tell — '

'My story?' grinned the woman. 'Nothin' like as eventful as yours, but we share one thing in common: I'm another on the run. That's right, runnin' from Johnstown, Moses Barton, that two-bit saloon and whorehouse of his, and bein' in the scumbag's pay as a . . . ' She hesitated, glancing away to the frosted window. 'Don't have to say it, do I?'

'I guess not,' grunted McGinley.

'Yeah, well, come the snows, Barton always ships a girl outa town to the miners keepin' guard on things up here. Winter comfort. This year, I drew the short straw. Been in these godforsaken mountains close on two months.'

Charley Branham paused a moment, easing the stock of the rifle to the floor, propping the barrel against the wall, then, with a toss of her long hair across her shoulders, continued, 'Anyhow, got to thinkin' that bein' up here might be the start of gettin' completely free, if I could fathom some way of comin' by a gun and a horse. Crazy, maybe, but anythin's got to be better than what I face back there in Johnstown. So, Barton sticks me in this shack and the minin' fellas keepin' guard pay their visits . . . 'ceptin' one ain't goin' home this mornin'.'

McGinley's stare widened. 'Yuh mean — ?'

'I mean, Mr McGinley, I killed him, early hours of this mornin'. Did it with a carving knife. Slit his flea bitten throat while he slept. Probably never knew a thing and died happy. His body's out back. Fellow by the name of Jules Dakins. A louse of the first order.'

Charley sighed, flicked at her hair with a steady, determined hand and gazed directly into McGinley's face. 'The Winchester there was Dakins. He arrived on a horse, but it must have strayed for warmth and cover. Weren't there when I dragged his body to the back.' She smiled mischievously. 'And that was my problem, 'til I spotted you up there on the track.'

McGinley swallowed carefully. 'Now you just hold on there, young lady,' he began. 'If you're plannin' on what I think yuh plannin' — '

'I join up with you,' interrupted

Charley on a snap. 'We ride out of here together.'

'T'ain't possible,' protested McGinley, 'not two mounted on one horse in these conditions, in this country. No, can't be done. Wouldn't make a mile before the mount collapsed. Out of the question.'

The woman turned and crossed to the window. 'I know this country,' she said quietly. 'Every track and trail of it. I could lead yuh clear of these mountains.'

'Not on one horse yuh couldn't. It's like I say — '

'I could also lead you clear of the miners hereabouts, and maybe we could help ourselves to one of their horses on our way. What yuh reckon?'

McGinley moved slowly round the table. 'Lady, I got more than enough trouble sweatin' on my back. I got Fake Morgan and Mart Peters gold-crazed and rattlin' like snakes in a basket. I got that godalmighty Moses Barton and doubtless a horde of his sidekicks primin' themselves up for fillin' me full of lead minute they spot a sliver of my shadow. And then there's the hangin' happy sheriff . . . I ain't one bit for leavin' yuh here to the minin' boys and Barton, but at the same time — '

'I reckon we got one of your problems headin' this way right now,' said Charley, scrubbing her fingers at the iced windowpane.

'Hell!' mouthed McGinley on a groan at the woman's side. 'The hang-'em-high sheriff and one of his sidekicks!'

12

'I got yuh spotted, mister. This is as far as yuh goin'. Might as well call it a day.' The sheriff spat defiantly into the snow, spoke quickly to his deputy and levelled his Winchester to a new grip in his hands.

'Didn't figure for me stayin' on yuh butt, did yuh?' he went on after releasing another fount of spittle. 'Well, yuh sure as hell read me wrong. Ain't never been known yet to back off from a hangin' prospect. And you, mister, are one-hundred per cent goin' to hang. You bet! Be the longest drop we've had in Remarkable in years. Tell yuh somethin' else . . . '

'What yuh goin' to do?' hissed the woman at McGinley's side, her gaze wide and anxious. 'There's two of 'em, damnit.'

'There a back way outa here?'

'Sure, but yuh ain't plannin' on — '

'I ain't leavin' yuh, don't fret,' said McGinley, checking the chamber of the Colt as he eased into the shadows. 'Yuh reckon you can keep them scumbags occupied and interested for a while?'

Charley turned slowly from the window. 'Mister, I been doin' that all my life! Couple of rats like them out there ain't goin' to be no problem.'

'Sorry,' nodded McGinley. 'Fool question. Leave it to yuh.'

'Thanks!' said Charley. 'Just you watch y'self.'

'You hearin' me in there, mister?' bellowed the sheriff again. 'Want yuh to know you're goin' to hang on two counts: the shootin' of Hank Green and the fella back there at the cabin where it seems yuh helped yourself. Double killin' gets special treatment in Remarkable. Want for me to spell it out for yuh?'

Charley shivered for a second as she slipped out of the long fur coat, adjusted her shirt and pants and tossed and patted her hair into place. 'Action!' she murmured to herself, watching McGinley leave the shack by the back door and close it softly behind him. 'Here we go — again!'

She glanced quickly through the window. The sheriff and his sidekick were still mounted, still staring at the shack, their rifles levelled from the hip, primed to blaze at the slightest reaction. She would need to make this in one, she decided, no messing, no hesitation.

'I ain't for sittin' here all day, mister,' began the sheriff again. 'Weather ain't exactly suitable. So I suggest we get to doin' this the easy way. Yuh just step through that door there, nice and quiet, hands high and no iron in sight. Yuh understand? And when yuh done that — '

The sheriff gulped, choked on his words, lost his voice, tried to spit and began to sweat. His deputy simply gawped and croaked. 'Sonofa-goddamn-bitch, a woman!'

'Top of the class for observation,

mister!' grinned Charley as she sidled through the door to lean provocatively on the wall of the shack, the fingers of one hand playing idly with a fall of her hair. 'Ain't seen either of you before. Yuh new hereabouts? Moses send yuh?'

'What the hell's a woman doin' out here, f'Cris'sake?' growled the sheriff, finally able to spit deep into the snow.

'Well, now,' smiled Charley easily, her gaze shifting quickly left to right for any sight of McGinley, 'yuh surely ain't expectin' me to spell that out, are yuh? You a full-grown man, and sportin' a law badge, too. Heck, mister, where yuh been all yuh life? This is minin' country, heavin' with big, big appetite miners . . . Yuh want for me to go on?'

'All right, lady, enough of the smart talk,' growled the sheriff again as his mount stamped and snorted impatiently. 'I ain't got the time for you or your talk. Yuh got a fella in there, a Wanted man, and he's all mine.'

Charley pushed herself clear of the wall and folded her arms across her breasts, at the same time stifling a shiver. Hell, she wondered, how long before McGinley made a move? 'Help yourselves,' she quipped, with a toss of her hair across her shoulders. 'Ain't no fella here.'

'He's here,' snapped the sheriff. 'That's the horse he killed for. Don't mess with me, lady. I come a long way and I ain't in the mood.'

'Horse ain't mine, that's for sure,' shrugged Charley, glancing at McGinley's hitched mount. 'Must've strayed here.'

'Oh, sure, and hitched itself!' scoffed the deputy. 'I heard some tall stories, lady, but not that tall. Try again, whore.'

'Who yuh callin' whore?' flared Charley, her arms falling to her sides. 'Yuh watch yuh lip there, fella.'

'All right,' croaked the sheriff, spitting again. 'Get in there, Sam. Go take a look round the place.'

'Yuh ain't been invited yet,' said Charley, as the deputy dismounted and trudged through the snow to the shack.

'Don't need no invitation from the likes of you, gal,' scowled the man, reaching the open door. 'Reckon yourself fortunate I ain't got the time for settlin' with yuh. Wouldn't be so smart time I'd finished.'

Charley stifled another deeper shiver. Where the hell was McGinley? She folded her arms again and glared at the sheriff. 'Yuh sittin' this out?' she mocked. 'That yuh style? Others do yuh dirty work? Ain't much of a lawman to my figurin'.'

'Don't push yuh luck, lady. I ain't normally a patient man.' The sheriff's gaze narrowed. 'What yuh see in there, Sam? Our man there?' He frowned at the silence. 'Sam? Yuh hearin' me?'

Charley slung her weight to one hip. 'Well, now, what's yuh fella found that's so intriguin' him, I wonder?' she grinned sardonically. 'Hope he ain't slippin' into my warm bed there! Best take a look for yourself, hadn't yuh, Sheriff? Feel free.'

The sheriff hawked, spat, tapped a

finger in his grip on the rifle and eyed Charley as if watching a slithering rattler. 'What yuh hidin' in there, lady?' he croaked.

'Me? Hidin' somethin'?' said Charley with a lift of her eyebrows and toss of her hair. 'Now what would the likes of me be hidin' in a place like this? Mebbe I got a dead body back there,' she added on a slow grin. 'Well, now, wouldn't that be somethin' . . . '

'Sam!' called the sheriff. 'What the hell yuh doin' back there?'

Precisely, thought Charley, with a quick sidelong glance to the shack door, just what was the deputy doing? Or perhaps she should be asking, what was McGinley doing?

The sheriff grunted, dismounted and made his way slowly through the snow.

★ ★ ★

Charley saw the shadow on the first glint of the sun. It spread across the snow from the sprawl of an outcrop like

103

a long, straightening finger, pausing for a moment, then reaching again and growing, softly, silently until there was finally a shape, the stark black silhouette of McGinley, Colt drawn and tensed in his right hand.

Charley shivered, her eyes widening, shifting from the sight of the approaching sheriff, to McGinley, dark as a spectre, at his back.

'Sam, damn yuh!' growled the sheriff, his footfalls flat and heavy. 'Will yuh just get yuh butt outa there? We ain't got all day.' He glared at Charley. 'I just hope for your sake, lady, that yuh ain't been playin' us along, 'cus if yuh have, I'm tellin' yuh straight up — '

'Don't waste yuh time, Lawman,' barked McGinley. 'Yuh partner's dead.'

The sheriff spun round, almost losing his balance, the rifle coming to a grip in both hands, his eyes narrowed to slits against the glare of the fierce winter sunlight.

'Knew I'd catch up with yuh sooner

or later,' he hissed, the rifle levelled at the hip.

'Short-lived, though,' snapped McGinley, the shadow from the sunlight at his back masking the grin that broke across his lips. 'Pity I ain't got the time to hang yuh. This'll have to do . . . '

And then the Colt spat, fast, accurate, unremitting, until the sheriff had been thrown back on staggering steps across the snow, his curses muffled to groans, the rifle falling from his grip, and he finally lay still like a dead bird of prey.

Charley had backed at the first spit of lead, her stare broken on the flash and crack, her body tensed and tight as the ice around her. Now, the stare fixed again on the body of the sheriff, and the shivering moving like tremors through her body, she could only gulp, wait for McGinley to move towards her, and hug herself.

'Hell,' she murmured, turning to follow McGinley to the shack, 'he never saw a thing.' She gulped again.

'Where'd yuh learn to shoot — ?'

'Get into somethin' warmer, then round up these rats' mounts,' ordered McGinley from the open door. 'Guns and anythin' else they were carryin' that might prove useful. We gotta move, and fast. All that shootin' here is going to be sweet music to some folks' ears. How long before yuh'd reckon on yuh first — ?'

'Customer?' frowned Charley. 'Never no tellin', but somebody's goin' to come lookin' for Dakins sure enough.'

McGinley grunted. 'Time's pressin'. Let's move.'

'What did yuh do with the lawman's sidekick?' asked Charley on another gulp.

'Took a leaf out of your book,' said McGinley, stepping into the shack. 'I slit his throat.'

13

They left the shack and the creek in silence, the scuff of hoofs through snow being the only sound to fall across that morning, the curls of breath swirling to the light from a burning, low-slung winter sun the only movement that might have attracted a watchful eye.

Their discussion of the destination had been brief and to the point.

'North?' McGinley had asked.

'Only choice,' Charley had nodded. 'Track's tough going, but if we make it to Morning Pass, we'll be home and dry to the plains' trail.'

'Then north it is. Where's Barton's miners holed-up?'

'Mostly round the main shaft and diggings at Longneck Peak. That's where the gold's stacked. And that's where yuh friends Mart Peters and Morgan'll be headin'. We can skirt round it.'

McGinley had grunted and gazed away in thought for a moment. 'Moses on the other hand, is sure to pick up my tracks to your shack, and when he gets there and finds — '

'Hell will be burnin' here on earth!' winced Charley. 'Like yuh say, let's move it.'

★ ★ ★

They were almost two hours along the track, with the morning fine and bright and the air invitingly warmer, when McGinley gestured to halt and pointed to a craggy ridge high above him.

'Pretty sure I saw a glow up there some place last night,' he said, scanning the heights. 'Miners, yuh reckon? Barton's men?'

'Miners still here this time of year spread themselves around,' said Charley shielding her gaze against the glare. 'But, yep, I'd figure for them bein' in Barton's pay. Ain't many who aren't.' She lowered her gaze to stare at McGinley. 'Not a deal we can do about 'em, but they're goin' to get real snappy when they spot me ridin' with yuh. Yuh thought of that?'

'I have. Have you?'

'Just another problem, eh?'

'Lady, when yuh got 'em stackin'up thick and fast as I have, what the hell's one more?' McGinley grunted, adjusted his hat, and urged his mount forward. 'Just so long as yuh can use one of them Winchesters we acquired when the time comes.'

'I know my way around, mister,' quipped Charley.

'Never doubted it for a minute,' smiled McGinley to himself. 'Nossir, never doubted it.'

Another mile climbing higher and they were forced into the darker twist of a narrow canyon where the rock faces rose sheer and ice-smooth at their sides and the shafted light from a cloudless blue sky seemed like a fearful onlooker.

Charley shivered, conscious of the sudden tension in McGinley's shoulders ahead of her, his tighter scanning of the rocks and the shadowed track.

'We clear this and we'll be through to the drift,' she called encouragingly. 'Whole sight easier from there on.'

'Needs to be,' grunted McGinley, but knew in the next ten seconds as they rounded a bend that nothing ever got easier, especially when three guns from three mounted men were ranged against you — and three pairs of eyes were saying only one thing:

Easy pickings.

★ ★ ★

'Barton's men?' hissed McGinley from the corner of his mouth, his hands already easy on the reins.

'Never seen 'em before,' murmured Charley. 'Scumbags driftin' through. Don't argue.'

'Clean out of arguments as it happens!'

They reined back sharply, Charley drawing level with McGinley's mount.

'Turned out nice, ain't it?' drawled

110

the bushy-bearded, black-eyed man at the centre of the trio.

'Better than I'd figured on,' leered the man to his left.

'And gettin' decidedly better,' sniffed the third.

'Oh my,' said bushy-beard, spinning his Colt through his fingers, 'we landed ourselves a female here.'

His partners tittered, holstered their guns and urged the mounts forward a step.

'Ain't that some luck, would yuh know?' mouthed one.

'I'd call it just that,' grinned the other. 'Fact is, brother Ely, in this sorta territory, this time of year, I'd call strikin' across a female a whole sight luckier than wakin' on a glow of gold blossom. What yuh say to that?'

'Come to think on it — '

'Yuh fellas wantin' somethin'?' asked McGinley, his stare as cold and tight as the ice-faced rocks.

'We wantin' somethin', Ely?' sneered the man.

'Well, now,' mouthed the brother, 'I'd be settlin' for the woman given the chance. And y'self?'

'Share and share alike, Ely. It's what we've always done. Can't be fairer.' The man turned to bushy-beard. 'What yuh reckon, Smarts?'

'I'd reckon on gettin' our butts outa this godforsaken country and rested some place warm,' glowered bushy-beard. 'So get to it, eh? Grab the woman and let's get ridin'.'

'Yuh heard the man,' shrugged Ely. 'What he says goes.'

'Yuh right there, Brother. Ain't never no arguin' to be done where our good friend Smarts is concerned . . .'

McGinley's gaze shifted quickly: to bushy-beard still toting a Colt, but loose and relaxed in his grip; to Ely and his brother, their guns holstered as they urged their mounts to a slow walk, confident of the cover from Smarts.

'Yuh ride like the wind when I move,' he hissed at Charley.

'Don't be a fool,' she hissed back.

'There's three of 'em, f'Cris'sake.'

'I can count, lady!'

'Not that good, yuh can't!' snapped Charley with a shrug of her shoulders.

McGinley tensed as his mount pawed the snow. 'Just do as I say, yuh hear?'

Charley pouted and gripped the reins.

The brothers came on at the same steady pace. Smarts' Colt still lay easy in his hand, but his eyes, McGinley noted, were alive and concentrated like a hawk's on a scurrying mouse.

'Scumbags,' murmured Charley almost below her breath. 'Hell, I can smell 'em from here!' she sniffed. 'How long they been in the saddle?'

'Too long,' mouthed McGinley, his grip on the reins sliding unseen to one hand. 'Time they were on their backs!'

'I'm tellin' yuh, mister,' began Charley, 'you try shootin' — '

But her protest was lost on the sudden swirl of activity: McGinley raised his mount to its hindlegs, at the same time drawing his Colt and, as the

113

horse snorted, whinnied and pranced to all-fours again, releasing two blazing shots, the first spinning Ely from his saddle as if pole-axed, the second spitting deep into his brother's chest to send him crashing to the snow in a whirl of limbs and spatterings of blood.

'Ride!' yelled McGinley, slumping low to his mount's neck. 'Ride, damn yuh!'

He heard the snort of Charley's horse, the slip and slither of its hoofs across ice, saw the flying snow around and between its legs, the flash of a gleaming eye, and then the glint of a Winchester barrel.

'What in hell's name!' he croaked, and winced at the exploding roar of the rifle shots that ripped through the canyon like thunder splitting the skies apart.

'Charley?' he shouted, coming upright in the saddle again as his mount stamped and circled frantically. 'Charley, will you just get the hell outa here before — '

'I got him!' yelled the woman, swinging her horse back towards McGinley. 'Fella with the beard, I got him. He's down. Dead, I hope!' She reined to a standstill, a broad smile setting her dark eyes alight. 'See, told you I could handle myself, didn't I?' she added, flourishing the Winchester to its scabbard. 'Did good enough yourself there, eh? Nice shootin', mister.'

McGinley had leaned forward in his saddle, his mouth open on a groan of exasperation, when he tensed again at the growling roar that engulfed the canyon and seemed for a moment to seep from the rocks like dragon's breath.

'Now we do ride, f'Cris'sake — for our lives!' he yelled at the top of his voice. 'Avalanche!'

14

The morning darkened under a curtain of grey ghostly light. The walls of the canyon closed in as if about to squeeze to death whatever life still lingered there, and the noise of the slithering, sliding snow high on the sloping ridges gathered and deepened until it seemed to McGinley it would burst through his skull.

'Ride!' he yelled again, urging his horse to greater speed, conscious of Charley a length ahead of him and the scumbag drifters' riderless mounts straining every limb and sinew for the opening to the drift at the far end of the canyon.

'Hell's teeth!' screamed Charley, glancing to where only moments ago there had been a canopy of cloudless winter-blue sky. Now there was nothing save the menacing swirl of snow under avalanche through which, like some half closed watering eye, the smudged sunlight tried to blink.

'Keep to a straight line,' shouted McGinley. 'Stay clear of the rocks.'

Charley's mount snorted, lost a grip on the frost-hardened snow, almost stumbled but regained its balance as she fell across its neck. So much for raging guns in a snow-locked canyon, she thought, daring herself to another skywards glance, wincing at the sight of the snow already tumbling in cascades of white breath from the ridges, seeming then to hang on the air in an eerie silence.

McGinley drew level and called to her: 'Just hold on and keep goin'. Don't stop for nothin', and keep yuh eyes dead ahead.' He slapped her mount's rump. 'Worst fall's comin' from the left. Follow me!'

He reined three strides clear, yelling encouragement to his mount, easing the reins to the straining muscles.

The first snow crashed to the ground

to his left, a second and third fall exploded in its wake; the rumbling deepened to a throaty growl; ice cracked and splintered; the light faded, grew brighter, faded again, lay above McGinley's head like some cold slab of rock.

Charley gasped. She was clinging to the reins and her mount's neck now for her very life, fearful that at any moment she would slide away to the ground, grovel in the snow, stay marooned until a fall buried her alive and still mouthing for McGinley, cursing Moses Barton and the two-bits vermin who had happened to be in the canyon on this day, at this time.

She gasped again, the breath thudded, it seemed, from her body, moaned, closed her eyes on the crash of falling snow, the roar of more to follow, and wondered if they would freeze her into blindness, or would she open them and see only whiteness like an endless light . . .

McGinley was at her side. 'Almost

there,' he shouted above the roars and crashes. 'Hang on there. And don't stop when we pull clear to the drift.'

'*If* we pull clear to the drift,' she yelled.

'We will!'

McGinley's voice rose again as he whooped to the mounts for one last effort, the final thrust that would bring them to the drift and safety.

More crashes, the roar deepened again to the very bowels of the canyon, and now, without warning, a wind, ice-tipped and cutting as a honed blade, began to whip into the riders' faces.

'Ride, damn yuh, ride!' screamed McGinley, and fell across his mount's neck, barely conscious.

★ ★ ★

Charley's eyes opened in quiet shadow and blinked on the glare of the fierce sunlight beyond it. She swallowed deeply, blinked again, and sighed. Was this the land where you came to rest after death? Where was it? Wherever, it was warm . . .

She snuggled into the folds of the bedroll blanket and lifted her face slowly to the warmth of the sun. Something here was familiar, she thought, her eyes half-open to the blurred shapes beyond her. Horses, saddled up, flicking their tails, snorting softly, waiting, or resting.

And beyond them, his gaze ranging slowly over the land, McGinley.

Charley leaned back on the rock face and shifted her butt to a more comfortable position on the boulder. Her eyes closed fully again and the images of the scumbag drifters, the shooting, the grey light and the avalanche flooded back in turmoil.

But she had survived, damn it, and this was not the land of the dead. This was Colorado, winter in the high mountains, and the fellow standing there was being hunted down by a whole pack of gold-crazy men. This was the harsh reality.

Her eyes sprang open like blinds at the sound of approaching steps crunching over the snow.

'We made it — just!' grunted McGinley, his gaze turning back to the canyon. 'No way in or out of there for a while, that's for sure.'

'Might be to our advantage,' said Charley. 'Anybody following our tracks might assume we never made it.'

'Mebbe, but t'ain't a diversion I'd recommend!'

'No,' murmured Charley, lowering her eyes for a moment. 'Sorry about that. Winchester raging in a snow-packed canyon ain't exactly good sense.'

'We need to move,' interrupted McGinley. 'Yuh feel up to it? Yuh were clean out there for a while.'

Charley took McGinley's helping hand to bring her to her feet, the bedroll blanket hanging loosely at her shoulders. 'I'm ready,' she grinned. 'And thanks for the blanket.' She adjusted her clothing, settled her hat. 'Any signs of Barton or the others?' she asked.

'All quiet — mebbe too damned quiet.'

'Avalanche would have raised hell for miles.'

McGinley's gaze scanned the peaks. 'That's what bothers me. Barton would have read it like a book. He'll know now where we're headin'.'

'We change direction?' frowned Charley. 'Could try headin' west after the drift. I heard tell as how there's tracks if you look close enough.'

'Well, mebbe,' said McGinley. 'Important thing now is to move. Put some miles behind us while we got the light. No sayin' when the clouds might pile in again. And no sayin' what they might be holdin'. Let's go.'

Charley looked back to the canyon only once as they began the long ride across the drift. She just wanted to be certain no one was following.

Not even the ghosts of those buried there.

The light stayed good, the sun held its warmth, the trail across the drift presented no particular difficulty so that the miles McGinley and the woman made until the early afternoon were also easy going and certainly, in Charley's reckoning, a more than welcome chance to recover from the avalanche.

In fact, she began to think, at this pace and if their luck held, they stood an even chance of making it across the peaks to sweeter, lusher grasslands to the west.

But it was a thought she had quickly dismissed. Nothing in her life had ever been that hopeful or easy. Best stick with the thinking of the man ahead of her, she figured. He called the shots — and pulled the trigger. Well, she smiled to herself, most of the time!

McGinley's thoughts were far from the prospect of lush grasslands, but never more than a glance from the snow-capped mountain peaks and the winter-locked lands below them. They had made good progress from the canyon; moved as fast as the conditions would permit without so much as a snag or slip along the vague track of the drift trail.

So why did he have this deep gut feeling they were being watched?

Nothing up there in the rocky sprawls and falls of the mountains to worry him unduly; no movements, no sounds, echoes, no glint of barrels. The mountains were bare save for the snow and ice — and the eyes.

There were eyes up there, sure enough, he could feel them on him: tracking him, watching, waiting. Patient eyes. But waiting for what, and when?

'We keepin' goin' 'til dusk?' called Charley. 'Best look out for some decent shelter for the night. And we're goin' to need fuel for a fire. Ain't a deal of spare brushwood up here.'

'I'm watchin' for it,' lied McGinley, flicking his gaze quickly from the peaks.

'Give it another hour, then we rein up.' He patted his mount's neck. 'How far this drift spread?' he asked casually.

'We get to holdin' to any sorta luck at all, we could clear it come noon t'morrow. One big downhill run from there. I'd figure for, oh, mebbe two days trailin' to the foothills. There's pine cover soon as we hit them.'

McGinley eased the pace until the woman drew alongside him. 'Yuh seem to know the country well enough,' he said. 'Yuh hail from hereabouts?'

'Small plains town by the name of Stockburn,' smiled Charley reflectively. 'Yuh won't have heard of it. Nobody has. Fifty miles west of here. Born there . . . hell, seems like two lifetimes ago.'

'So yuh goin' home?' murmured McGinley.

'That's the plan, if I make it, and if there's a home still to be had. My folks have long since passed on. Had a brother there, though, but I ain't heard of him since . . . Yeah, well, a long whiles.'

She shrugged under the hugging coat. 'And you, mister, where are you headin'?'

'Over and out of these mountains in one breathin' piece is about as far as my reckonin' goes right now,' grinned McGinley, scanning the peaks again. 'Just that, lady. No more, no less.'

★ ★ ★

Charley slept peacefully and deeply in the warm glow of the fire beneath the rocky overhang flanking the main trail of the drift.

She had said no more of Stockburn or why she had left and found herself one of Moses Barton's girls in a ramshackle mining town. And McGinley had not asked. She had guts, she could shoot and she could look to herself on a hazardous trail. It was not for him to probe deeper. And certainly not on this night. There was too much at stake. Not a deal of time for sleeping either if they were going to be moving again at first light.

Keeping watch was going to make it a long night, thought McGinley, adding more fuel to the fire, especially when there were other eyes still out there.

And all of them wide awake.

15

Somewhere, between the timeless state of dozing fitfully and waking with a sudden start and jerk, there were voices. Two of them at least; strange, lost voices that seemed at a distance, never closing, low and muffled as if caught on some quickening wind. Voices that should not have been there . . .

The crack of a spark in the low-burning brushwood fire brought McGinley back to the real world with a twitch, a grunt and a rush of light to his eyes that almost blinded.

'The dozin' fella wakes,' mocked a voice lightly. 'Easy there. No goin' for that iron, mister. Blow yuh head apart before yuh laid a finger to it. Just take it steady. Yuh ain't goin' no place — not yet yuh ain't.'

McGinley glanced quickly at the tight, huddled shape of Charley, still sleeping the sleep of the exhausted.

'I see yuh met up with our Charley gal there,' added the voice again. 'Some woman, eh? Or ain't yuh sampled her delights yet? Too busy runnin', were yuh? Just how far did yuh figure on gettin'? Hell, we been watchin' yuh for hours. Could've taken yuh long back.'

'We?' frowned McGinley, squinting at the blurred, half-lit bulks only yards across the snow, caught in the fading glow of the fire, the lifting darkness of night and the breaking wink of first light. 'Who are yuh?' he croaked, shifting against the already creeping cold.

'Me, I'm Clem Dragge. My partner here is one by the name of Pieces Cooper. Both of us in the employ of Mr Moses Barton. You'll have heard of him, o'course.' The man grinned and eased his Winchester across his bulging gut.

'So what now?' croaked McGinley again. 'Yuh here for breakfast, or is this visit official?'

'Don't get smart, mister,' threatened

Cooper, taking a step forward. 'Yuh done enough damage back there in Johnstown. You'll be answerin' to that to Mr Barton in person. Meantime, yuh wake that sleepin' whore and get her on her feet. Time we pulled out, eh, Clem?'

'Too right. Shift, fella. Now!'

McGinley struggled wearily to his feet, adjusted his coat and hat and was about to move to wake Charley when she stirred, sensed instantly that something was wrong and was upright and glaring at Barton's henchmen in seconds.

'Hell,' she groaned. 'Might've known. The rats are out!'

'See yuh ain't lost nothin' of yuh spirit, Charley,' grinned Dragge. 'Must be all that killin' yuh got yourself into back there at the creek shack. Throat-cuttin', eh? Poor old Jules. Wouldn't have taken yuh for a blade type. Better watch m'self in future.'

'Don't fret,' sneered Charley, 'there ain't no chance of you layin' a finger to me again. Same goes for yuh rat partner there.'

130

'Yuh might be singin' to a different tune come noon,' said Cooper, spitting into the snow. 'Bear it in mind. Now, let's shift.'

'Where we goin'?' snapped Charley.

'Mr Barton's got a real hankerin' for seein' the pair of yuh,' leered Dragge. 'Anxious, he is, like he can get when he's angered and riled. Know that well enough, don't yuh, Charley?' He smiled and tapped the Winchester. 'He's waitin' on us at the main shaft. Two hours' ride.'

McGinley glanced quickly to the breaking light in the east. No hope there, he reckoned. Day was going to come up bright and cloudless. Not a chance for now of bad weather setting in.

'Go along with 'em,' murmured Charley at his side. 'These scum shoot soon as spit on yuh.'

McGinley nodded and moved to the mounts.

'Best you unbuckle that gunbelt, mister,' drawled Cooper. 'Right there. Yuh ain't goin' to have need of it again.'

They trailed fast across the packed snow, holding hard to a track that headed first from the drift to a long, narrow creek, then higher to where steeper shelving rock faces and clusters of boulders marked out the land as mining territory. The morning broke clear and fiercely sunlit, the cold air biting but strangely invigorating after a night of being huddled into blankets by a smoke-heavy fire.

Dragge led the party, with his rifle-toting partner bringing up the rear, leaving Charley with the opportunity from time to time of closing on McGinley to speak to him.

'Main shaft where we're headin' is way off our trail,' she hissed, after the first half-hour of riding. 'Gold's stored there 'til the weather clears and they ship it down to Johnstown. Up to a dozen of Barton's men guarding it. Barton don't normally visit this early. Must be anxious to meet yuh!'

'He's anxious!' muttered McGinley.

'Yuh figure for them other rats, Peters and Morgan, headin' out here?'

'They will if they're desperate enough — and they're desperate. Men are where gold's at stake.'

'Supposin' . . . Hell, what's the point! We ain't got a deal goin' for us, that's for sure. Yuh got any ideas?'

'Clean out of them right now, lady! Ask me come midday, assumin' I'm still here to ask.'

They trailed on in silence.

★ ★ ★

'Get that woman out of my sight! I'll deal with her later. Leave the man — McGinley, did yuh say? — I want him here.'

Moses Barton drew long and deep on the fat, heavy cigar in his fingers, blew the smoke to a shaft and then to a shimmering haze. He grinned, and flashed his hawkish gaze to McGinley as two of his gathering of sidekicks dragged Charley deeper into the depths of the cavern.

'Didn't take much tracking down, did yuh?' said Barton, as the smoke cleared to the cavern's mouth and the bright, cloudless day beyond it. 'Nobody leaves these mountains 'ceptin' on my say-so. Yuh should remember that, Mr McGinley.' His henchmen murmured their agreement. 'Now, let's get to decidin' how we're goin' to deal with you, shall we?'

McGinley blinked on the gloom, the smart of cigar smoke across his gaze, sniffed on the dank aroma and shifted his boots across the dry rock floor. Find a way out of this if you can, he told himself on a swallow. Damn the day he had ridden into Remarkable!

'Got a whole lot busy back there in my town, didn't yuh?' Barton went on behind another drift of cigar smoke. 'Very unhealthy, 'specially with the shootin' of my good friend, Chems. Most unfortunate. Oh, sure he had his faults — ain't we all? — but shootin' him down like that . . . My, my, that's a hangin' offence, Mr McGinley. A hangin' offence.'

The henchmen murmured again and stared like a pack of waiting wolves at McGinley.

'Same goes for the death of my man, Luke. Hell, he weren't doin' no more than an honest night's work. Ain't that so, boys?'

Barton blew a perfect ring of smoke. The sidekicks grunted and stared.

'And not content with that,' said Barton, his gaze narrowing, 'yuh then had to go messin' with the delectable Charlotte, not to mention the killin' of a lawman and his deputy on my premises. Now *that* is serious business. Tell the man, Sam.'

A rolling-bellied man with a bristling ginger moustache stepped from the group of watching men. 'Nobody, not nobody, messes with Charley,' he growled, clenching his hands to rock-like fists. 'And nobody, 'specially the likes of you, mister, gets to grabbin' her for himself. Does that, and he's lookin' down a dozen barrels. And mebbe a whole lot worse.' He glanced at Barton. 'I say we execute this scumbag right now.'

The sidekicks grunted their approval on raised, threatening voices.

Moses Barton drew on the cigar, blew a ring and watched it hover like a noose over McGinley's head. 'See what I mean, fella?' he said on a twisting grin. 'Feelin's run high where our Charley's concerned.' He paused a moment. 'I guess we passed the death penalty on yuh. Yuh got anythin' to say?'

McGinley turned his gaze to the cavern's mouth again and eased his weight to one hip. 'If I take the trail west, how long before I hit the border? You fellas help me out here?'

The rolling-bellied sidekick thrust his bulk forward. A man stepped to his side and spat across McGinley's boots.

'Hold it there, boys,' urged Barton from a swirl of smoke. 'Fella rates himself smart. Well, let him reckon so.

We'll show him somethin' different in our own good time, eh? Meanwhile, go secure him, Sam. Yuh know where.' He glared at McGinley. 'Yuh just made one helluva nasty bed for yourself there, mister. Don't envy yuh when this pack gets to work!'

McGinley could only twitch and squirm against the trickle of icy sweat down his spine, and turn his gaze from the dazzling sunlight to the darkness of the depths of the cavern.

He was about to be swallowed alive.

16

They dumped McGinley — suitably roughed up, kicked and beaten for his 'smart-ass talk' — in a cave once used for storage, and bolted the solid wooden door behind them as they left. As far as McGinley was concerned they might never be coming back.

Or perhaps they would, he reflected, as their footfalls faded, the silence settled and a thickening darkness closed in. They would have to find some amusement through the long, cold hours.

He took a deep breath, listened for a moment, half hoping to hear Charley's voice, but was glad then that the silence stayed unbroken (what could he do even if she was close by?) and ran his hands along the walls.

Hard, dank rock, he thought, as his fingers spread across the pitted surfaces. Same went for the floor and the rough, crusted ceiling. Nothing here to inspire a fellow into thinking he might escape. Only one way out — and he was leaning on it right now: the solid door.

He took another breath, grimaced on the stink of stale air, the pain in his bruised body, grunted and closed his eyes to the darkness.

Where, in this labyrinth of passages, caves and shafts, were they holding Charley, he wondered, and just what had Barton in mind for her as a punishment? He swallowed. Did he need to answer that?

How deep were they storing the gold? How soon before they moved it? Was that wholly dependent on the weather? He took another breath. Perhaps more to the point where the gold was concerned, how long before Mart Peters, Fake Morgan and whoever else was riding with them reached the mining area?

McGinley's eyes opened slowly. He blinked, listened, licked at a cold beading of sweat on his upper lip, flexed his fingers, then relaxed. Time to conserve the energy, he decided. Take it easy; let the pain ease. No panic. Listen to the silence. Wait for it to break.

And when it did, be ready to shift faster than the spider there crossing the back of his hand.

*   *   *

McGinley lost track of time, save to surmise that it must still be daylight out there on the mountains and the fierce, blood-red winter sun was still shining. He had tried reckoning on the passing of an hour, and given up; counted down the seconds to a minute and figured he was heading nowhere.

He had relived the events of the night in Remarkable, his escape to the mountains, the discovery of the body in the cabin, Johnstown, the shoot-out in the livery, Chems Parton, the hanging-crazed sheriff, Charley, the avalanche . . .

And he might have gone deeper,

140

recalling the detail of what might have been, might still be, when he heard the first scuff and crunch of approaching steps.

One man, heading his way. Would he stop at the cave, unlock the door, open it, step inside . . . ? The sweat was glowing on McGinley's face by the time the man finally paused, put his hand to iron and slid the bolt.

'Out yuh come, fella,' drawled the voice. 'Boss wants yuh. Figurin' on yuh fate, I guess. Tell yuh straight up, I wouldn't wanna be standin' in your boots.'

McGinley waited a moment, the door partially open to the vague lantern light of the passage leading back to the main drift. He needed the man to step closer. Just another few feet . . .

'I'm talkin' to you, fella,' drawled the man again. 'Don't tell me yuh gone to sleep in there. Shift yuh butt, will yuh?'

The man shuffled the few fatal steps, peered into the depths of the cave and probably felt no more than the grip of cold fingers on his neck, the tightening bite of them, before the rush of blood to his head, behind his eyes; the pounding that grew to a torrent; the stifled gurgle; the sudden flash of a strange white light, and then darkness and oblivion.

McGinley bundled the body to the back of the cave, stripped the fellow of his gunbelt and Colt, buckled it to his own waist, and bolted the door firmly as he scurried, like the spider, into the gloom.

★　★　★

He waited in the nearest shadows. No sounds, nothing moving. The fellow must have come alone. Fine, that was just fine, thought McGinley, wiping the sweat from his face, his tight, narrowed gaze taking in the passage, the spreads of darkness beyond the blurred lantern light.

Which way? Back to the entrance, or deeper into the mine? No, his first priority had to be the woman.

He tensed at the sound of men's voices, laughter, footsteps approaching then passing and fading, veering away into another passage. McGinley waited for the silence to settle again before easing to the rock-face wall as he followed in the direction the men had taken.

He went carefully, two or three steps at a time; pausing, waiting, listening, conscious of his aches and pains, the slightest movement, the merest sound, his right hand never more than a flicker from the butt of the holstered Colt. The men somewhere up ahead of him were silent now, lost in the maze of shadow-filled passages, caves and shafts. How deep should he go, he wondered? It would be only a matter of time, one wrong turning, a slip into some unseen shaft, before he was lost or came face to face with a clutch of Barton's men.

He paused again, sweating in spite of the chill dampness. He had passed into a narrower passage with a low ceiling, lit by fewer lanterns, the floor littered with dust and smaller rocks. An area, he guessed, not much used, perhaps abandoned, or a dead-end. But it was lit and he was certain the voices and steps had faded in this direction.

He flexed his fingers, took a deep breath, blinked in the gloom and the ache that burned at the back of his eyes. Time to move on, go deeper, at least as far and as deep as the faint light would permit.

He had taken a single step from the shadow when he heard the scuffle somewhere up ahead. He melted back to the darkness, waited, listened. More scuffles, muffled voices, and then, like some sudden crack of a whip, Charley's outburst of curses.

'Damn yuh, sonsofbitches! I'll see the pair of yuh in hell! Keep yuh thievin', scumbag hands off there!'

There was a growl from one of the men, a fit of tittering from the other, more scrapes, thuds, grunts.

'Get a hold of her, will yuh?' sneered a voice. 'What's with yuh, can't yuh handle the bitch?'

'What do yuh think I'm tryin' to do here, mule-head?' grunted a second voice.

'Well, you just keep it easy, yuh hear? Boss don't want her marked.'

'She'll be marked time I've done with her — and it won't be no bruisin' neither! Give me a hand here, will yuh? Grab her other arm, f'Cris'sake . . .'

McGinley tensed and twitched against the tingle of sweat. He could step out of the shadow, Colt drawn, levelled, aimed, and blow the two men into eternity, do it and not waste a scratch of lead — only trouble being, he would bring Barton's men charging down the passage like a plague of rats.

So could he get to the woman without firing a shot?

The scuffles, grunts, curses were closer now, Charley obviously resisting and protesting every inch of the way to a prospect she had probably imagined a hundred times. Moses Barton would not be much for compromise.

He drew the Colt gently, slowly from its holster, weighed it in his hand, glanced along the gleam of the barrel, then tensed as the shadows of the struggling men and Charley leapt ahead of them.

'I said to keep yuh scumbag hands off me!' spat Charley.

'There'll be more than a hand across yuh if yuh don't do as yuh told. Damnit, the varmint just bit me!'

'And her with such pearly teeth at that! Would yuh credit it for a handsome looking woman the likes of our Charley? Why, I tell yuh — '

The barrel of McGinley's Colt whipped across the back of the man's head before he had taken another breath. His grip on Charley loosened, slid away, his eyes bulging, legs buckling at the knees.

'What the hell — ?' growled his partner, turning, his attention on the woman broken as he saw for just a flashing second the butt of McGinley's gun heading for the centre of his face.

There was the crack of bone, a groan, a spurt of blood. The man, blinded and spinning into a surge of darkness, fell forward, grovelled for a moment and groaned again under the thud of McGinley's boot.

Charley had spun back to the rock wall, her stare wide with a mix of fear, anger, surprise, the shudders running through her body like tremors in a quake.

'Which way?' hissed McGinley, lifting Charley to her feet.

'Hell, mister, how in the name — ?'

'No time! Which way?'

'Back to where they were holdin' me,' gulped Charley. 'There's an old drift shaft, brings you out higher up the mountain.'

'Yuh sure?' frowned McGinley. 'We ain't got space for mistakes.'

'It's there, and if it's open — '

'*If* it's open?' snapped McGinley. 'What yuh mean?'

147

'The weather; snow and ice. Could've blocked it.'

'Chance we're goin' to have to take. Grab a lantern from the wall there and let's shift.'

They disappeared into the darkness like shadows returning to it.

17

Fake Morgan picked at the droplets of ice frosting his stubble and flicked them from his fingers to the snow. His gaze and concentration tightened on the sprawling mass of high peaks, the blue of the clear sky behind them, the ball of blood sun and the deep, stiff shadows that seemed to clutter the land like bodies. Another time, another day and he might have been grateful to be alive among the awesome splendour of a Colorado winter. As it was, he was growing impatient, highly suspicious, and the cold was creeping into his bones.

And he was not best pleased with his partner either.

'Well,' he grunted, flicking angrily at another droplet, 'yuh decided? This the place or ain't it? We ain't here for the scenery.'

Mart Peters shifted in the saddle to the roll of his mount's flanks. 'Could be it's the place,' he said casually, raising a hand to his eyes against the sun glare. 'I'd reckon it could well be. What yuh reckon, Mr Coon? This what we're looking for?'

The sidekick drew his mount level with Peters. 'I trailed this way before,' he reminisced, rubbing his chin. 'Long back, o'course. Must've been thirty-eight, time I was ridin' along of Billy Slaughter and Pete Mackay. I ever tell yuh about Billy? Hell, he was some fella. I recall the time he shot — '

'We ain't interested in your memoirs, mister!' sneered Morgan. 'Yuh got somethin' useful to say, say it.'

'I been up here,' grinned Wilbur on a noisy click of his tongue. 'Sure I have. Mine shaft's to the east. Longneck Peak' — he jabbed a mittened hand at a far peak — 'to yuh right. That's where they pull the biggest seams.'

'Yuh sure about that?' grunted Morgan.

' 'Course I'm sure. Came this way with the Hunter boys, thirty-nine, hell of a Winter. Yuh know somethin', I seen snow deeper than — '

'Yeah, yeah,' snapped Morgan, 'bet yuh have at that. Just hope yuh memory's a sight better than yuh identification!'

'That fella posin' as Frank Boyd — '

'Let's leave it, shall we?' ordered Peters. 'I ain't for hearin' any more about Frank Boyd, Chems Parton or the likes of 'em. They're the past. We got the now and the future, and it's the future and snafflin' fifty thousand in gold from under Moses Barton's nose that concerns me. So, is that range to the east where we should be?'

'That's it, Mart,' said Wilbur, clicking anxiously. 'I swear to it.'

'Me too,' added Mr Coon. 'Seein' it now, right there, I do indeed recall Billy Slaughter sayin' as how them mountains were a pot of gold. Longneck Peak, right there. And them were his very words.'

Peters shifted again to his mount's restive roll. 'Fair enough. I go along with what yuh sayin'. What you reckon, Fake?'

Morgan picked the last droplet of ice from his stubble, flicked it to the snow and trailed it with a fount of spittle. 'Tell yuh what I reckon,' he muttered. 'I reckon as how it's a whole lot strange we ain't seen a sight or track of Barton or that fella we mistook for Boyd since we left Johnstown. And what was all that gunfire and sounds as close to avalanche as I ever heard all about? Anybody answer me that? And while you're ponderin', get to figurin' what we're goin' to do should it be that Moses Barton and a whole horde of his minin' scumbags happen to be right there in them mountains right now.' He spat again. 'That's all I got to say — savin' to add, just in passin' yuh understand, that I don't like all this silence. T'ain't natural, not even up here.'

Nobody, it seemed, had noticed.

152

Moses Barton thrust his hands deep into the pockets of his long fur coat and glared from the mouth of the cavern over the sweep of the snowswept Colorado mountains. The bright, burning sun cast his long shadow back to where his men were gathered, silent, watchful and not a little fearful of the tirade that was about to erupt.

'I don't do it m'self, it don't get done,' he murmured to himself. 'Ain't that so? Ain't that always been so?' He turned slowly, his hands still buried in the coat, the light like a blaze of flame behind him. 'So what the hell I pay yuh for, eh? Pay yuh to *not* do things; to foul 'em up, make a whole steamin' hash of whatever yuh touch? That what yuh here for?'

The men shuffled uncomfortably, stared at their boots, looked away, anywhere but at Moses Barton.

'Don't have a lot to say, do yuh? Not

none of yuh. Well, that ain't so surprisin'. What is there to say, 'specially now with the birds flown, pair of 'em, and us standin' here like idiots? Empty-handed idiots.' He spat deliberately, noisily before delving for his cigar case, making a selection, lighting it and curling a thick cloud of smoke to the ceiling. 'One man, one woman. Just that,' he continued, eyeing the men again. 'Not exactly a force to be reckoned with, eh? Not an army. Should be simple enough to hold 'em prisoner, shouldn't it? Hell, *only* one man, *only* one woman.'

He blew another cloud of smoke, watched it drift and curl, twist and thin to a soft vapour trail. 'But what do you scumbags manage?' he growled. 'Why, yuh manage to let 'em get away, escape, vanish so we don't rightly know where they are, and ain't likely to, not 'til yuh get yuh butts shiftin' and get to doin' somethin' about it, and fast, before I have a mind to start slicin' off yuh ears, one by one — '

'Best take a look back here, Mr Barton.'

Moses swung round in a wreathing curtain of smoke to face Clem Dragge. 'Well?' he clipped. 'What the hell now?'

'We got company driftin' this way. Four of them gold-diggin' vermin from Johnstown — Peters, Fake Morgan and two others.'

'Headin' up here?' grunted Barton.

'No doubt about it,' said Dragge, gesturing from the mouth of the cavern to the sweep of the creeks and valley far below him. 'See for y'self.'

Barton came to the henchman's side, the cigar clenched tight between his teeth, the smoke drifting round him. He stared, grunted, removed the cigar and spat. 'Let 'em keep comin'. It's goin' to be a rough climb.' He smiled. 'Be all worn through when they get here, won't they, Clem?' The smile twisted behind more smoke. 'Keep me informed, and keep watchin'.'

The men shifted uncomfortably again as Barton turned back to them.

'And what the hell are you lot waitin' on?'

'We were kinda wonderin', Mr Barton,' ventured a tall man anxiously.

'Kinda wonderin' . . . That's your whole trouble, ain't it? Standin' about wonderin' when yuh should be doin'. Wonderin' ain't gettin' us nowhere, is it? T'ain't likely to neither.'

'Yuh want for us to get lookin' for Charley and that fella she's tied in with?' asked the man.

'Well, now, that'd be real smart thinkin', wouldn't it?' mocked Barton. 'Real smart.' His facetious grin faded. ''Course I want yuh to get lookin' for 'em, yuh dumb-head! Now! And don't go foulin' up again. And don't go announcin' yourselves all over these mountains. Do it easy, discreetly. Yuh understand? I ain't askin' too much, am I?'

The men murmured disgruntedly and began to turn away.

'And double the guard on the gold,' growled Barton to the men's backs.

'Wouldn't want to lose that, would yuh?'

★ ★ ★

Save for the scuff of hoofs through snow, the occasional clip where one struck a half-buried rock, the splintering of ice and the men's grunted encouragement to their mounts, the silence had remained tight and heavy as if holding the day in its grip.

Fake Morgan had been listening to it for close on an hour and heard nothing that had settled his instinctive wariness. But he had seen something — and that was almost as worrying.

Somewhere up there, high in the sprawling mass of rock faces and the gaping mouths of caverns, he had seen a glint, a movement, an unnatural shift of shadow. No freak twist of the light, he had reckoned; nothing made by bird or beast. No, this had been made by a man, or perhaps more than one.

Barton and his men? Very likely, he

figured. Already at the main shaft, watching and waiting. Not good. Too many of them to take out in a straight gunfight; damn near impossible on the snow and ice-gripped slopes of a mountain in the middle of winter!

He would wait, he had decided, until they had climbed higher before calling Peters to hold up and assess the situation. Meantime, there was the mystery man Chems Parton had first crossed in Remarkable. Who was he? Where was he? Lost in the wastes of an avalanche, or was he up there on the mountain? Perhaps he would be the next movement to watch for?

Or was he the silence?

18

'What yuh see, McGinley? What's up ahead?' Charley spat grit and dirt from her mouth, wiped a grubby hand over her sweat-streaked face and raised the lantern higher to cast its flickering glow over the cavernous darkness.

McGinley paused where he lay sprawled on the shelving of stones and rocks and blinked into the shadowy drift of the passage. 'We're goin' higher, that's for sure. But there's more fallen rock to come. Looks as if the whole shaft collapsed at some time.' He coughed on a swirl of dust. 'Yuh sure this is the way?'

'It's the only way, mister! What's back of us don't bear thinkin' about.'

McGinley grunted and blinked again. 'How we doin' for light? That lantern goin' to last?'

'I'm prayin' so,' said Charley, examining

159

the wick. 'Looks good enough for now, but we need to keep goin'. Any hint there of an opening comin' up?'

'Not yet there ain't. And frankly — '

'Don't say it, McGinley. Don't even think it,' urged Charley, moving closer. 'Let me lend a hand there. You take the lantern.'

McGinley shuffled back over the rocks and dirt, raising a dust cloud as he went. 'Hell,' he mouthed, taking the lantern from Charley. 'If I'd have figured that night in Remarkable . . . If I hadn't holed up at that damned cabin . . . ' He spat and knuckled the dust from his eyes.

'If's a mighty big word, mister,' grinned Charley. 'And I should know. The devil I should! Still, that's another story and it ain't a spit of use at the moment. So let's get to it. Hold the light higher . . . '

* * *

'Know somethin', McGinley?' said Charley an hour later, as she slumped among the rocks. 'I reckon any man who spends better part of his good days cooped up in a place like this, shiftin' muck and stone and Godalmighty stubborn rock, deserves every nugget of gold he finds. I tell yuh, it just ain't worth it! Remind me never to buy a mine.' She shook the dust and dirt from her hair. 'Your turn,' she grinned. 'We're makin' headway, though.'

'Sure,' said McGinley struggling forward, 'but how much longer before Barton's rats get to scuttlin' this way? They get a whiff of where we are, we're as good as dead — or mebbe worse if the old man's in a bad mood.'

'You can bet on that for a certainty,' said Charley, relaxing, as she watched McGinley take up the work. 'Don't take a deal to rile Moses Barton at the best of times. This little caper will have him jumpin'!' She wiped her hands down her pants. 'And no thanks to me neither. But I ain't goin' back to Johnstown, that's for sure. Sooner die where I am than find myself back there.' She tossed her hair to her neck. 'Yuh got my full permission to shoot me, mister, if it comes to it. And don't miss, yuh hear?'

'I hear,' grunted McGinley, rolling back another rock. 'But I don't reckon it's comin' to that, not if we — '

'Hold it, McGinley,' said Charley urgently, the sweat beading and gleaming on her face. 'Hold it right there and turn very slowly . . . very, very slowly. Look at this.'

McGinley turned without disturbing so much as a pebble, his gaze wide and round-eyed and then narrowing as he watched the lantern flame flicker like a nervous dancer.

'Tell me I ain't mistaken, mister,' murmured Charley. 'That flame is doin' what it's doin' because there's a draught of air somewhere. And it ain't at my back.' She swallowed. 'So if it ain't at my back, it's gotta be — '

'Up ahead,' clipped McGinley, turning again to face the shadow-streaked depths of the cavern, peering for the merest hint of a glint of light.

'Yuh see anythin'?' hissed Charley, bringing the lantern closer.

'Not yet,' gasped McGinley, struggling over the rocks and stones. 'Keep the light high . . . Right there . . . Forward a mite . . . Hold it! Don't move.' He scrambled higher, the sweat trickling down his cheeks to drip through his stubble, his boots levering him on, slipping, sliding, gripping again as he heaved forward.

'Yuh got somethin'?' muttered Charley.

'I got it,' said McGinley. 'It's here. A way out. Only trouble bein', is it frozen on the outside? Can we shift these last rocks?'

'We'll die in the darned effort!' snapped Charley crawling to his side.

★　★　★

'How long we been ridin' t'gether, Mr Coon?' asked Wilbur, easing to the pick and prod of his mount as it felt for a secure hold. 'I'd reckon it for, well, now

. . . gotta be all of ten years.'

'And some,' mused Mr Coon. 'How come yuh askin'?' he added with a puzzled glance.

' 'Cus I just been thinkin' here as I'm watchin' and tryin' to stay saddled on this hell-track through these godforsaken mountains, as how this might well be our last ride t'gether.'

Mr Coon spat deliberately over a sun-splashed rock face. 'Hey, now, Wilbur, that ain't no way to go talkin'. I ain't never heard such hogwash twaddle. How'd yuh come to such fool thinkin'?'

Wilbur's tongue clicked rapidly behind a rush of saliva. 'I'll tell yuh, Mr Coon, sure I will. I came to this profound conclusion 'cus I got one helluva gut-twistin' feelin' that there's guns up there in them peaks just waitin' to pick us off when the time comes. Simple as that.'

'Well, now, ain't that somethin'?' said Mr Coon, his gaze tight on the narrow trail ahead. ' 'Cus it just so happens I've had much the same feelin'. It's a fact. Honest up, no kiddin'. Ain't that some coincidence?'

'It is that, Mr Coon, it surely is,' said Wilbur, shortening the rein. 'So what we goin' to do about it?'

'I figure,' whispered Mr Coon, 'that we pull out, first chance we get. Leave the gold to Mart and Fake. Could do with the money, sure we could, but, hell, t'ain't worth dyin' for. We'll make it some place else — alive! Agreed?'

'Agreed, Mr Coon,' nodded Wilbur. 'We pull out soon as . . . ' He squinted ahead. 'Like now? Will yuh take a look at that!'

* * *

The crunch and crack of rock snapping free of frost and ice, the groan of a boulder beginning to topple, the slide of dirt and stone, split the silence of that Winter day like hammer blows to the head of a giant chisel.

A hawk screeched madly and flapped

165

into soaring flight from the higher peaks. The rumbling roar of rock spooked mounts and brought a handful of Barton's henchmen scurrying to the mouth of the main shaft.

Far below, on the winding creek trail, Mart Peters reined back sharply, a look of amazement at the sight of the tumbling rocks creasing his weathered face.

'What in the name of — ' he began, but choked on his own voice as the slide of snow and stone and dirt gathered momentum.

'That fella — McGinley,' croaked Morgan. 'It's him. He's up there!'

Moses Barton, standing at the main shaft, bellowed inaudible orders to men who either did not hear him above the roars and rumbles, or chose to remain deaf.

'Will somebody f'Cris'sake do somethin'?' he screamed into space.

Clem Dragge fired a volley of useless lead into nowhere. Pieces Cooper drew his Colt but let it hang loose and heavy in his hand.

'McGinley and Charley — they've broken out of number two shaft,' he shouted. 'Hell, they could set a whole landslide goin' if them rocks at the mouth break clear! Yuh see that, Mr Barton?'

' 'Course I see it,' bellowed Barton. 'I ain't blind! Go get the sonofabitch. Kill him, any way yuh like! Yuh hear me? And bring that whore to me. I'll deal with her personally. Do it, damn yuh!'

Back on the creek trail, Wilbur called to Mr Coon that now might be as good a time as any to pull away. Mr Coon agreed and had already reined his mount round to the distant sprawl of the drift when Fake Morgan growled like a bear and thudded a fist into his face.

'Don't even think about it, either of you,' he snapped. 'I'll shoot the first man who turns his back on me.'

Wilbur opened his mouth to protest, but thought better of it. Mr Coon could only lick at the blood from his bleeding nose and stare at the still tumbling rocks.

'Barton's men are up there,' yelled Peters. 'They've seen us.'

'Seen us long back,' growled Morgan. 'Best we can do for now is hole-up in cover 'til this is over. Let's do it!'

There was another roaring crash of rocks, a swirl of dirt and dust as the side of the mountain seemed to splinter and erupt.

The hawk screamed and soared.

★　★　★

Charley spat, blinked, spat again and clawed her way over the rocks to McGinley's side. 'Fresh air!' she gasped blinking again on the sunlight as she took a long, deep breath.

'Don't get to relaxin',' said McGinley, easing higher from the tumbling rocks. 'Give me yuh hand. This ain't no place to wait around.'

'Where we goin'?'

'Them scumbag gold-diggers are down there,' McGinley indicated, drawing Charley to him. 'And Barton and his rats are lookin' decidedly mean. We got one gun and no hope of gettin' anywhere near horses. Not exactly a bristlin' prospect.'

'Say that again,' sighed Charley. 'But at least we ain't trapped in no mountain.'

'True,' said McGinley. 'Just trapped on it! And mebbe not even that if we don't soon move.'

'Higher?' gulped Charley.

'Higher. So just don't slip, all right? It's goin' to be a long way down!'

The screaming hawk swooped above their heads, its screeches splintering through the roar of more tumbling rocks.

19

Clem Dragge waited for the dust cloud to clear, wiped the grit of it from his face and dared to shift his already numbed limbs into life where he crouched alongside Pieces Cooper in the rock cleft.

'What yuh see?' he grunted. 'They moved yet?'

His partner spat the dust from his mouth and narrowed his gaze. 'They ain't where they were, so they must have.'

'They ain't comin' down,' murmured Dragge. 'Must've gone higher, damnit.'

'I ain't much for heights 'specially in this weather,' said Cooper. 'Don't much fancy climbin' up there.'

'And I bet yuh don't much fancy goin' down neither — not if yuh gotta face Barton! That ain't no prospect, is it?'

Cooper spat again. 'Mebbe yuh right. And I ain't much for tanglin' with Peters and Morgan. Yuh can bet they're still waitin' down there.'

'So don't look to be much of a choice, does it?' Dragge eased a shade higher. 'Rocks have stopped fallin'. We'd best move. Yuh want me to lead?'

'You lead. But what's the plan? How we handlin' this?'

'Don't figure for Charley bein' too much of a problem. She'll simmer down once we've taken care of that fella, McGinley. So we go for him first. No messin'. First sight yuh get of him, yuh shoot. But don't, f'Cris'sake, hit Charley. Boss wants her in one piece.' Dragge grinned as his eyes gleamed. 'And so do we, eh? Think about that and you'll never notice how high yuh are. Come on, let's climb.'

Cooper swallowed and began to sweat in spite of the whip of the mountain wind.

* * *

Moses Barton selected and lit a fresh cigar, blew the smoke across the wind and scanned the spread of the land below him. He could see the tracks clear enough, trace exactly the line Peters and Morgan had been taking immediately before the rockfall.

But spotting where they were holed up now was nothing like so easy.

Their tracks had petered out at a cluster of outcrops and boulders that reached like a long, bulging limb towards the main trail to the mine shaft. They could be anywhere in there, thought Barton, inhaling deep on the cigar. Just anywhere; just waiting, watching.

Let them, he reckoned. He had the edge on the higher level, and he had the guns. And if he could trust to Dragge and Cooper taking care of McGinley and bringing the woman to him still unmarked . . .

He swung round quickly, a cloud of cigar smoke swirling above his head.

'Harry,' he called to the mouth of the

172

cavern, 'yuh get y'self out here, will yuh? We got some details to talk through.'

He waited patiently, drawing calmly, thoughtfully on the cigar, his gaze tight, determined, settled.

'Yuh want me, Mr Barton?' croaked an old, wizened man, shuffling from the cavern like some sleepy-eyed lizard. He yawned and scratched irritably at the snow-white strands of his beard. 'Hell, that was some rock shift we had back there. Reminds me of a time out the Yukon way — '

'I'm sure it does,' grinned Barton. 'But t'ain't that I wanted to discuss. We got a more pressin' consideration.'

'Oh,' said the old man, scratching again, 'and what might that be, Mr Barton?'

'Yuh been my number-one teamster more years than I care to recall, and where wagons and horses and shiftin' 'em are concerned, I'd trust yuh all through.'

'Well, that's real nice to hear, Mr

Barton,' smiled Harry, 'and much appreciated. Always done my best by yuh, that's for sure.'

'And much appreciated too.' Barton blew smoke to a twisting ring. 'So,' he began again, 'if I were to say to yuh what's the chances of rollin' out a wagonload of gold today, what would be your considered opinion?'

'Wouldn't need no considerin', Mr Barton,' said Harry, folding his arms, dramatically. 'I'd say yuh were plumb crazy to even figure for it this time of year with the weather about as predictable as a drunken whore and the trail outa here as grim as it gets. True enough, we got the wagon up here and the team like we always have, but they wouldn't make a mile, never mind the trail all the way to Johnstown.'

'I wasn't thinkin' necessarily of Johnstown.' Barton examined the glowing tip of the cigar. 'I was thinkin' more of the easier drift trail out to the plains.'

'The drift trail?' frowned Harry. 'But how come yuh'd wanna . . . ' He winked and nodded. 'You schemin' on out-foxin' them scumbags down there?'

Barton's gaze tightened. 'Could it be done, Harry? Today? For an additional consideration to your good self, naturally.'

'Well, now,' said the old man, scratching through the strands of his beard again, 'if you're reckonin' on what I figure yuh for reckonin', and if we could sorta talk this through fully for a while, well, mebbe we could hit that trail come the afternoon and before the sun gets tired.'

'Good,' grinned Barton, offering a cigar to Harry. 'So let's talk, shall we?'

* * *

Fake Morgan turned his back on the menacing, snowcapped bulk of the mountain and concentrated his gaze on Wilbur and Mr Coon.

'I hope,' he said slowly, his breath spinning on a white shroud, 'that I'm readin' your intent all wrong. Tell me I am, Mr Coon. Tell me we ain't been wastin' our time trailin' this far in this Godforsaken weather all to no avail just so's you and Wilbur here can turn tail when it suits. T'ain't so, is it?'

Mr Coon blinked and swallowed in one contortion of muscles. 'Hell, no,' he spluttered. 'Not put like that it ain't.'

'Is there another way of puttin' it?' drawled Morgan. 'My eyes ain't deceivin' me, are they? You were all set to pull out back there, minute that rockfall sprung across us. Yuh sayin' now as how yuh weren't?'

'I'll tell yuh the fact of it,' clicked Wilbur. 'Ain't no point in lyin' about it. Fact is, Morgan, this trek out here to get our hands on that gold ain't goin' one bit to plan, savin' that we're here. And that ain't exactly healthy with Barton and his guns ranged up there and that fella we mistook for Boyd still on the loose. And, don't go f'gettin', only the four of us.'

'That's it,' snapped Mr Coon. 'That's just it. Too many guns and us down here. It don't look good. Yuh gotta grant that much. And how long we goin' to be holed up here? If we ain't made a positive move come dusk, we'll freeze to death. And that's another fact of it!'

'My, my, them heads of yours have sure been workin' some for once, and there's a fact for yuh,' sneered Morgan. 'Well, now, puttin' it as yuh have, mebbe yuh should pull out. Save yuh skins. Why not? Hell, the smell of 'em's been plaguin' me and Mart for weeks! So, sure, go ahead. Pull out. Right now. Yuh in agreement there, Mart?'

Mart Peters prised himself from his lookout cleft in the boulders, blew hot breath into his fingers and flapped his arms across his chest. 'Do what the hell yuh like as far as I'm concerned,' he croaked icily. 'Couldn't give a damn. But before yuh get to scurryin' like rats, yuh'd best note that Barton's now got two men on the mountain huntin' down that fella, McGinley, and the woman with him, and there's some wizened old sidekick just trailed a wagon and team out of the main mineshaft.' He blew harder across his fingers. 'What do you reckon on that? Any opinions?'

'Well, now,' began Wilbur, 'I'd figure — '

'Plain enough, ain't it?' said Mr Coon, blinking excitedly. 'Barton's readyin' up to shift the gold. He's goin' to load the wagon and risk the trail to Johnstown.' He paused thoughtfully for a moment. 'But, hell, that's some risk in this weather.'

'*If*, my friend, it's Johnstown he's headin' for,' smiled Wilbur.

'Damnit,' frowned Mr Coon, 'yuh mean — '

'Fascinatin' prospect, ain't it?' said Peters, stamping his feet. 'But let's suppose Barton pulls out with a full force of his men ridin' gunshot to the wagon, which ever way he goes he's goin' to have to skirt round mountains. Now, this time of the year, it ain't goin' to take a deal to block a trail at almost any point. And once we got the wagon and Barton and his men penned tight as hogs, well, gentlemen . . . We'll be pickin' 'em off like flies, won't we?' He thudded a fist to the palm of his other hand. 'So, who's for pullin' out, or who's for a spot of mountaineerin'?'

Nobody moved or said a word.

★ ★ ★

Charley gasped, scrambled her fingers on the frosty rock ledge and heaved herself the few inches needed to gain a firmer foothold.

'Hold it there,' wheezed McGinley from above her.

'Easier said than done, mister,' gasped Charley again. 'I ain't sure whether I'm holdin' on here, or frozen to the darn mountain! How much higher?'

McGinley squinted against the whip and sudden swirl of the wind, the glare of the sun, his body tensed and ice cold; arms, legs, fingers and toes beginning to feel as if they were no longer a part of him.

'Another few feet,' he gasped. 'There's a wider ledge and some sort of cleft. Might be a cave.'

'We still got company?' hissed Charley, as if expecting a body to appear at the side of her.

'They're still there,' said McGinley. 'Startin' to climb. We get to the ledge, we might be able to pick 'em off before Dragge down there gets trigger happy.'

Charley tightened her fingertip grip and winced at the agony of it. 'So don't let's hang about, mister. Just keep movin', eh?'

McGinley grunted and climbed on.

It was another ten minutes of heaving, gasping, reaching for every frost-tight hold before he finally slapped a hand on the ledge and clawed his fingers to a tenuous grip.

He drew himself painfully on to the ice-streaked surface and had turned and stretched to haul Charley to him when the first of the gunfire ripped through the wind and splattered the rock at his back.

20

'Did yuh get the sonofabitch?' Pieces
Cooper peered into the haze of the
glaring sunlight as he struggled to hold
to his perch on the rocks. 'Hell, no yuh
didn't,' he mouthed. 'He's made it to
the ledge, damn it.'

'I can see that, dumbhead!' snapped
Dragge from the cleft above him.
'Might've missed, but the fella ain't
goin' no place, is he?' He grinned, spun
the empty chamber of his Colt and
reloaded with a quick flick and dance of
his fingers. 'Can't risk goin' much
higher, can he? And he sure as hell
can't come down — not and stay alive.
I'd reckon that for bein' trapped. We'll
pick him off in our own good time.
Charley'll come down when she sees
the way of things and the night closes
in.'

Cooper grunted, blinked against the

glare as he shifted his gaze, but did not have the guts to look down. He swallowed and just wished this whole mess would be over quickly. It had been bad enough climbing this high; there would be no going higher, certainly not for him, and as for going down . . .

He blinked again on the blur of a sudden flurry of movement far below him.

'What the hell's goin' on down there?' he called to Dragge. 'Am I seein' things? That Harry bringin' up the team and wagon?'

'That's just what it is, my friend,' said Dragge, already peering intently at the scene at the main shaft. 'Looks very much to me as if Moses is plannin' on shippin' out the gold right now. He ain't goin' to wait for the weather to improve.'

'Risky, ain't it?' frowned Cooper. 'What's he want to go doin' that for? We ain't never shipped gold this time of year. T'ain't all his to ship anyhow. Other miners got a say in what happens to their efforts, and when. And this ain't the weather. Old Harry's thinkin' must be turnin' to sawdust.'

Dragge was watchfully silent for a moment. 'Them gold-hunters see what's goin' on and they're goin' to reckon it their lucky day,' he murmured. 'Barton loads the wagon, puts it to the trail . . . Hell, all they gotta do is wait!'

'Goin' to be one helluva haul into town.'

'If that's what Barton's plannin',' grunted Dragge. 'Don't make no sense, so it's time we weren't here. We finish the fella up there, grab Charley and get ourselves back to the shaft. Whatever's festerin' in Barton's mind, we're going to be a part of it. We ain't missin' out. Agreed?'

But right then Pieces Cooper had no stomach to agree anything.

★ ★ ★

Wilbur clicked his tongue through a splattering spray of spittle, wiped the back of his hand across his mouth and eased closer to Mr Coon. 'See that,' he hissed into his partner's ear. 'Yuh seein' what I'm seein'?'

'I'm seein' it. Every last detail.' Mr Coon shrugged his shoulders beneath the sprawl of his fur coat. 'What yuh reckon?'

'One man handlin' the team — no youngster at that — Barton and a handful of his cronies ridin' shotguns. T'ain't goin' to be too difficult.' Wilbur's tongue lapsed into a clatter of clicking. 'More worryin' is that fella up there on the mountain. McGinley ain't for bein' taken easy. Still, we can't concern ourselves with everybody, can we? We'll stick with Morgan and Peters for now. If there's a bag of gold for the liftin', we'll be there. But not if it gets rough.'

'I ain't for mixin' with flyin' lead,' said Mr Coon, adjusting his hat. 'It gets too damned dangerous. Get y'self killed keepin' that sorta company.'

'Tell that to McGinley!' clicked

Wilbur. 'But he wishes right now he'd stayed along of us, eh? As it is . . . Shame, but I can't think of no finer epitaph than a simple Amen.'

'Amen,' echoed Mr Coon.

*   *   *

'Don't leave it too late before yuh draw that Colt, will yuh, mister? I don't wanna die up here.'

Charley backed deeper into the rock cleft and watched anxiously as McGinley checked the chamber of his Colt. 'Down to survival shots,' he mouthed. 'Goin' to have to think of somethin' else.'

'Somethin' else?' gasped Charley. 'Ain't much of a choice of *something else* up here, is there?'

McGinley eased as close to the brink of the ledge as he dared to take a quick look into the crags and reaches below him. 'Mebbe not,' he murmured, 'but we can't go wastin' shots on slim chances of a hit.'

'Them scum still climbin'?'

'Only one of 'em now.'

'That'll be Dragge,' said Charley, wiping her windswept hair from her face. 'Cooper ain't much of a stomach for anythin' risky. He likes the quiet life. He won't shift.'

McGinley eased back from the brink. 'Don't change our situation none. We can't climb higher. We can't go down, at least not yet. We've got to somehow . . . ' He paused, rubbing his chin thoughtfully. 'That boulder there, other side of this cleft — yuh reckon we could shift it?'

Charley eyed the vast, frosted bulk. 'Shift that?' she swallowed. 'Mister, I don't reckon our muscle power would be any better than a breath on a piece that size. Any case, hidin' to nothin' it's frozen solid.' She glared at the bulk and tossed her hair defiantly into her neck. 'But yuh right, we gotta try. Let's try!'

McGinley risked another glance from the rim of the ledge to check on the approaching, stretched and sweating

186

shape of Dragge. He still had some way to come and was fully committed for the moment to the safety of every hand and foothold, watched by his pale, twitching partner who looked as if he might pass out on the next swish of the wind.

'We got some while yet. Best not waste it,' hissed McGinley as Charley crawled towards the boulder. 'We push with our feet, backs to the rock face. Soon as yuh hear a crack, feel a shift, ease up. Don't want yuh goin' down with the bulk.'

'Mister, we get to easin' this the width of a hair, it'll be a miracle — and I'll be prayin'!'

★   ★   ★

'Yuh figured yet the trail they'll be takin'?' grunted Peters, his gaze tight and unblinking on the activity outside the main shaft above him.

Fake Morgan shielded his eyes against the sun glare. 'I'd swear to it they ain't figurin' on Johnstown. Barton's goin' to head for the drift, mebbe work his way down to the plains. Once he hits that, he can head where he likes.' He spat angrily. 'Why's he doin' that?'

'Yuh friend Parton mention anythin' before he got himself killed?'

'Nothin'. Not a word.'

'Way I see it, is the way I wager you're thinkin' it — he's plannin' on helpin' himself to the gold, every last nugget of it. Sees his chance, don't he? Half a year's work there, all done for him. Never had to break sweat. Now he's got men scurryin' round McGinley like flies to bad meat, and he don't figure on us bein' a threat, leastways not 'til he's clear. So, he figures, what's to stop him?' Peters tapped his fingers across the rock. 'But it ain't goin' to work, not if we shift now and get ahead of Barton at the drift. What yuh say?'

'I say we do it. Move fast. Goin' to be a while before Barton's all loaded and movin'. All the time we need to set an ambush.'

Peters nodded. 'And that fella, McGinley, what about him?'

'What about him?' shrugged Morgan. 'He's out of our hair. Stuck up there on a mountain, ain't he? Ain't goin' no place, savin' a cold grave when the time comes. We forget him.'

Peters nodded again, unsure for a brief, fleeting moment if McGinley was the sort of man you ever quite forgot.

Or who would allow you to forget.

★ ★ ★

McGinley grunted, winced, sweated and thrust his boots once again at the 'obstinate, sonofa-goddamn-bitch' boulder until it seemed his legs would splinter and crack and his back twist into knots. 'Hell!' he croaked, glancing quickly at Charley alongside him, her body similarly contorted, thrusting and straining with the effort to shift the boulder.

189

And so far, she sighed inwardly, the 'fool thing' had refused to yield so much as a sliver of the frost and ice that fastened it tight to the ledge.

'Kick at the ice,' croaked McGinley over another grunt.

'Yuh got it,' called Charley, aiming her heels at the base of the boulder.

She kicked for a minute, kicked again, harder and in the frustration of anger, then eased back, her hair matted in the sweat across her brow and in her neck.

'Don't want to worry you at a time like this,' she groaned, her eyes opening and closing like a wind-blown shutter, 'but you may not have noticed that Barton's on the move down there.'

'What yuh on about?' mouthed McGinley through his grunts and curses.

'Barton's drawn up the mine wagon. I figure for him loadin' the gold and pullin' out. Mebbe he's got some scheme of his own in mind.'

'Yeah,' grunted McGinley, 'mebbe he

has at that. Mebbe it's been there all along. But right now, I got other pressin' matters . . . '

He cursed through a hiss of angry breath as his boots flattened on the boulder and the muscles in his legs took up the strain.

'Kick, will yuh? Kick for yuh life. Mine too, while you're about it!'

It was another five minutes before they heard the creak and then the crack of splintering ice and the 'sonofa-goddamn-bitch' boulder began to move.

21

Pieces Cooper's eyes had filled with images that made his blood run cold, his ears with sounds that confused and bewildered his already addled brain. But there was a new sound, sudden and menacing, that shut out all the others and needed no fathoming.

Somewhere — but a whole sight too damn close for his liking — the earth was beginning to shift, or at least some part of it; right there, higher up the mountain, not a body's length from where Clem Dragge clung to the rock face like a frozen fly.

He shivered, held his breath, tightened his clawing grip, and saw the boulder on the ledge begin to move, to and fro in a slow, crunching, rocking motion.

'Clem!' he yelled. 'Yuh see that, above yuh, the boulder? It's shiftin', f'Cris'sake!'

How long it took for the nightmarish truth to dawn on Clem Dragge would be hard to tell. Cooper had watched the man stiffen in his precarious hold, caught a glimpse of the terror clouding his eyes, the colour draining from his face, his mouth open as if to call out, shout, or maybe spit a final curse.

But the sound, the shattering crack and splintering of rock from frost and ice, had drowned whatever sound the fellow might have made, and in the next moments — as the boulder finally left the ledge in a shower of smaller rocks rushing behind it — spun Dragge from the rock face to a swirling, twisting body crashing to frozen ground below with the screams echoing to the peaks long after the fatal thud.

Fear, sheer terror, nerve-ends shredded to a broken web, gripped Pieces Cooper even as the outfall of the boulder fell across him like a hail from Hell.

Seconds later, he too lay dead in the winter loneliness of the Colorado mountains.

★ ★ ★

'That wagon ready to roll?' yelled Moses Barton above the roars and rumbles of falling rocks, the creaks and crackings of shattered ice.

'Almost, Mr Barton,' returned Harry, the teamster, as he wrestled with the tack and horses growing wild-eyed and more frantic by the second.

'No 'almost' about it,' shouted Barton. 'It's ready. You men there, saddle up and ride shotgun. Get the wagon to the drift — and yuh don't stop for nothin', yuh hear?'

'This fall keeps up there won't be no trail,' scowled one of the sidekicks, his gaze tracking the tumbling rocks.

'Just do it for once, will yuh?' screamed Barton, throwing aside a half-smoked cigar. 'How many times do yuh need tellin', f'Cris'sake?'

'There's still some gold to load up,' called another man. 'Yuh want we should — ?'

'No time,' yelled Barton again. 'Leave

it. Just move before the trail's closed up. Now!'

'Mebbe we should wait,' said a henchman, struggling to help Harry with the fractious team. 'Mebbe the fall will ease.'

Barton ground his heel across the still smoking cigar. 'Yeah, and mebbe hogs'll fly!' he growled, drawing his Colt from its holster. 'Next man who questions my orders, is a dead man.' He levelled the gun menacingly. 'And I ain't foolin'.'

A cloud of swirling dirt, dust and snow swept across Barton's glaring, blood-veined gaze, but could not hide it.

* * *

'Wagon's movin',' said Mart Peters, nudging Morgan where they crouched behind a sprawl of boulders. 'It's gettin' ahead of us. Mebbe we should hit it now.'

'No, not yet. Too many guns,'

grunted Morgan. 'Wait 'til it reaches the drift. We'll take a shorter cut — through those rocks there.' His gaze moved to the higher peaks. 'That fella, McGinley, sure is a whole lot troublesome. Where the hell's he disappeared to now?'

'Any luck he's got swept up in that fall he started,' murmured Peters.

'Not him,' mused Morgan. 'Too smart for that. You see the fella, Mr Coon?'

'Not a hint. He's gone. That woman along of him I shouldn't wonder.'

'Never mind McGinley,' urged Wilbur on a sudden clicking of his tongue. 'Who cares? Let's just keep close to that wagon, eh?'

Peters adjusted his hat and grinned. 'Gettin' gold itchy, my friend? Feel it fidgetin' in the palms of yuh hands, can yuh? Bad sign. Yuh can start gettin' careless with an itch like that. You watch it now, fella.' His grin faded and the gaze slid to shadow. 'Better still, *I'll* watch yuh.'

'Where to?' gasped Charley, pressing herself tight to the rock face on the ledge. 'I guess we could say we're all through here.'

'More than,' said McGinley, clearing the sweat from his face. 'We got lucky, so we cash in on it fast. We need horses.'

'Looks as if Barton's pullin' out completely. He'll take all the mounts he can lay a hand to.' Charley shivered and hugged herself against a sudden whip of the wind. 'Nothin' of those scumbags who were tryin' to reach us?'

'Only bodies,' murmured McGinley, peering intently at the far end of the ledge. 'They should've gone back while they had the chance. Darn fools.' He eased a step along the rock face. 'This ledge eases away to a drop to smoother goin'. If we could make it down there . . .'

'There's a back entrance to the main shaft,' said Charley. 'Mebbe we could find it — and if we're still gettin' lucky, we might be in time to help ourselves to horses before Barton's all through.' She tossed her hair. 'And then?'

McGinley's gaze stayed steady and thoughtful. 'Shiftin' that boulder got Barton's sidekicks off our backs, and the fall may have delayed his movin' the gold, but not by long. We may still have a chance of collectin' some mounts — fact is, we got to if we're goin' to clear these mountains in one piece.' He paused a moment. 'Meantime, there's Peters and Morgan waitin' down there, and we know what's on their minds.'

'There's goin' to be some fast lead flyin',' said Charley, then pushing herself fully upright and flicking her hair to her neck, added, 'Even so, we're still here, mister, still breathin'. Yuh gotta give us that! So let's see just how far we can take it from here, eh? Yuh game, Mr McGinley?'

McGinley tapped the butt of the Colt. 'Glad to share your optimism, lady!'

They waited until another fall of rocks and ice had slid down the mountain to the creek trail, grinned quietly at the sounds of Barton's bellowed curses, then eased away to the far end of the ledge and judged how best to begin the long descent to where Charley reckoned the miners' mounts were hitched.

The going over the first thirty feet of rock, frosted stone and smooth, icy surfaces where the packed snow lay only to deceive the unwary step, the careless reach for a foothold, was heavy and precarious. But slowly, foot by foot, ridge by ridge, boulder to boulder, they began to descend, silently and, more to the point on this side of the mountain away from the cavernous entrance to the main shaft, unseen and unheard.

'They got anybody guardin' the hitch-line?' asked McGinley in a moment of pausing for breath.

'Mostly,' said Charley. 'Usually one of the older hands posted lookout; sometimes along of Harry, Barton's teamster, but I figure for everybody bein' concerned with that gold and the wagon to be botherin' overly with a line of horses. We might just make it.'

They moved on; more careful steps, uneasy footholds, fingertip grips that left their hands numb and cold, and always, as the day wore on and the high blood sun began its slide behind the peaks to the West, with an increasingly whippy wind that McGinley feared might well blow in another snowfall. They had to have horses and be saddled up no later than dusk.

He had merely grunted at the thought and moved on again.

★   ★   ★

Four horses — loose hitched; two of them saddled — perfect, thought McGinley, laying a hand to Charley's arm where they crouched in a heave of boulders by the main shaft's back-door.

'Luck's holdin',' he murmured, his gaze still tight on the mounts standing easy and relaxed.

'But somebody's got plans for 'em,' whispered Charley, brushing her hair from her cheeks. 'Where's Barton?'

'No sign. Must be with the wagon. Mebbe he's pulled out with it.'

'Yuh can bet to that! Won't let it out of his sight,' huffed Charley on a sudden shiver. 'We should move, eh? Get ridin', mebbe clear the main stretch of the drift come dark. Could be in the pines by — '

'Hold it,' hissed McGinley, the hold on Charley's arm tightening. 'We got company. Ease back. Let 'em move in. Not a sound.'

Two men, both armed, the fellow to McGinley's left a paunchy, rolling hulk with a ruddy face and a half-smoked cigar clamped between his nutmeg teeth, the other, taller and much younger, his hat pulled low, hands tight in his pockets, his gait more a swagger than a walk. A young gun, thought McGinley, who obviously rated himself in any company, anywhere, even out here.

'Yuh fancy playin' yuh part again?' whispered McGinley on a quick glance to Charley. 'Sorry to ask, but it might help.'

'I read yuh. Leave it with me,' murmured Charley. 'But not for too long, yuh hear? I ain't for dallyin' with either of them scum.'

McGinley watched, tense and anxious, as Charley patted her hair into a tidier heap, adjusted her shirt and pants and grew from behind the cover like a body appearing on the swish of a magician's wand.

She smiled and sidled to the track with the provocative assurance she might have brought to crossing a crowded bar.

'Well, now, look who I've come across,' she soothed. 'How yuh doin', boys?'

The paunchy fellow drew the half-smoked cigar from his teeth and spat across a snow-topped stone. 'Charley, as ever was,' he grinned. 'Ain't you a sight for sore eyes. Got half the fellas hereabouts lookin' for yuh, so how come — '

'Yuh hold it right there, lady,' sneered the younger man, his Colt already drawn and levelled.

'That ain't no way to treat a girl,' said Charley, her gaze suddenly colder and anxious. 'Thought yuh'd be happy to see me.'

'Sure we are,' grinned paunchy again. 'You bet. Why, I was only thinkin' earlier — '

'Where's the man — that fella, McGinley?' grunted his partner. 'He still with yuh? I ain't seen nothin' of him in a while. He get put out of his misery up there?'

'Hey, now, ease up there, will yuh?' smiled Charley, glancing quickly to the cover, wishing McGinley into action. 'Gettin' carried away some, ain't yuh? All the questions. So happens me and that fella got separated soon after . . . ' Move McGinley, move, she thought. 'Soon after that rockfall.'

Charley was conscious of the movement at her back, the softest crunch of a careful step, then the slip and slide of a shadow. She stiffened, froze, her fingers clenched and crushed to tight fists, and stared into the unblinking eyes of the younger man.

She knew and could hear what was coming even before McGinley's gun had blazed, spinning the Colt from the younger man's grip as he fell back and then doubled, groaning and clutching at his gut, as a second shot ripped into him.

The paunchy man's mouth opened, his fingers trembled, the half-smoked cigar dropping to the snow where it hissed for a moment as the fellow spun round, slipped, regained his balance and rolled on pumping legs back to the main shaft.

'Let him go,' said McGinley, collecting the dead man's Colt and tossing it to Charley. 'We take the two saddled mounts. Yuh know a back track to the drift trail?'

'I know it,' she gasped, still reeling from the spit and roar of the gunshots, the sight of the mouthy youth dying in front of her. 'But somebody will have heard the shootin'.'

'Too right,' grunted McGinley. 'Which means, as of now, we ain't here!'

22

'Yuh hear that? A Colt gettin' busy. Blanket to a bedroll that's McGinley, back of the reach there.' Fake Morgan's gaze narrowed on the sweeps of rock and mountain crags as he reined his mount to a halt on the rough track trail. 'He's loose and active. Could spell trouble.'

Mart Peters relaxed his grip on his reins and eased to Morgan's side. 'Don't fret none. Only thing interestin' McGinley right now is gettin' his hands on a horse and ridin' out fast as he can. He ain't goin' to take on Barton. Too many guns. McGinley ain't dumb.'

'That much I've figured,' grunted Morgan. 'And that's what bothers me.'

'Forget it,' grinned Peters. 'Leave the fella to himself. We got an appointment with gold. How close are we to the drift?'

'I reckon for less than a half-mile,' clicked Wilbur, pulling his collar tight to his neck against the chilling wind. 'We clear that draw there and we should hit the drift well ahead of Barton.'

'That wagon still movin'?' asked Morgan.

'It's left the mine shaft,' said Mr Coon from the rear of the track. 'Goin' slow, but it's movin'. Barton'll make it.'

'Yuh reckon for him waitin' on a sight of McGinley and the woman, if she's still with him?' frowned Peters. 'He ain't goin' to live easy with the thought of Chems' killer goin' free.'

Fake Morgan spat deep into the snow. 'Mebbe not, but Barton's figurin' on livin' a whole lot easier on the comfort of a wagon load of gold. I wouldn't take bets on his priorities.'

'So we move on,' gestured Peters, reining to the head of the line. 'And just for safety's sake, we keep an eye open for McGinley. But if we spot him, no drawin' attention to ourselves. We got our own priorities.'

* ★ *

Moses Barton glanced anxiously at his long-serving teamster working the wagon horses, and relaxed. Got to hand it to old Harry, he thought, put him behind a team and that is where he stayed, regardless of anything or anybody.

Chances were he had heard the shooting same as they all had, and he had doubtless figured the cause of it and wondered who had got the better deal on the draw. But seeing as how there had been no sight of Barton's men since the echoes faded, he had probably drawn his own conclusions. Which also maybe explained the silence among the men riding shotgun.

Barton drew angrily on the freshly lit cigar and scanned the peaks above him. Nothing at the moment; no hint of McGinley and the woman, but you could wager real gold they had got themselves horses and were on the move. Question was: would McGinley interfere or head fast for the safety of the pines and the distant plains beyond?

He drew on the cigar again, reined his mount to the wagon and called to the old-timer. 'How we doin', Harry? Not so bad, eh? Trail here's a sight easier than I figured.'

'We keep this up and we'll be on to the drift and crossin' it well before dark,' said the teamster, leaning to the clutch of leather in his grip.

'Good,' grinned Barton, the cigar glowing across his teeth. 'That's what I like to hear, somethin' positive. Stay with it, Harry, I reckon for us — '

'That said,' added the old man, tightening his grip in a grunt of encouragement to the team, 'I ain't takin' one bit to the thought of McGinley loose in them mountains. We lost Dragge and Pieces, mebbe others, and we still got them gold-grubbin' scum sittin' somewhere on our butts.'

The teamster hawked and spat across the wind. 'I can handle my job up here, Mr Barton, and it don't fuss me none knowin' what I'm haulin'. I'll get this outfit to the drift for yuh, no sweat. Anywheres yuh say. But you gotta make certain we got a clear run: no guns, no shootin'. This team spooks in these conditions and I ain't answerin' to the consequences. Think on it.'

Moses Barton was already thinking — deep and fast and hard. He was also watching.

★ ★ ★

'Hell,' mouthed Charley reining her mount into the steeper rock cover of the mountain track, 'of all the double-dealin', fast cheatin' scumbags, he's got to be number one.' She pulled angrily at the loose reins. 'I got it figured now — oh, my, have I just! Yuh see this down there, McGinley?'

McGinley halted his mount some yards ahead of the woman and reined the horse alongside her. 'I see it,' he murmured. 'Moses Barton makin' off with the spoils of other men's graft. It surprises you?'

'It surprises me to think he thinks he can get away with it, damn him.' She pouted stubbornly and tossed her hair. 'Can he?' she added, glancing quickly at McGinley.

'Ain't exactly a platoon ranged against him, is there? Who's goin' to stop him? Who's got the guns?' McGinley shrugged against the nip of the thinning air. 'Light's beginnin' to fade. Another hour and he'll be almost clear of the drift and headin' into easier cover. Men'll go with him when they realise there's a gold share-out in the offing. It's in the nature of things.'

'Well, I ain't for lettin' the sonofa-bitch ride out of here with all that money,' snapped Charley. 'That I ain't! Damnit, he owes me three months' pay!' She pouted again. 'I'm for collectin'. We come this far, we got

211

guns, horses . . . Yuh goin'to help me, mister?'

'Lady, yuh gotta be clean outa yuh mind to even think — '

'Yuh don't have to o'course. Just keep ridin' and I'll understand, but I ain't startin' a new life wherever it might be without bein' able to pay my way. Hell, if I can't do that, I'll be back in the first two-bit saloon in the first town I hit.' Charley's gaze on the slow-moving wagon below her narrowed and focused. 'Know somethin', it wouldn't take a deal to spook that wagon team . . . What yuh reckon?'

★ ★ ★

The light was low and fading, the late afternoon sky filling with a tumbling mass of cloud scudding on a brisk north-easterly, and the winter snows high in those Colorado peaks and across the plateau of the drift scarred by already deepening shadows, when somebody let loose the mayhem and the chaos erupted.

Mr Coon, buried in the cover of boulders, his coat pulled tight about him, collar snuggled to his neck, figured for the noise beginning somewhere among the frozen peaks. Wilbur, on a nervous click at his side, pointed to a snow slide gathering speed and thickening on a slope facing him.

'Didn't get started on its own, did it?' he had hissed. 'That lot hits the wagon, there won't be no wagon never mind the gold!'

Mart Peters had begun to fidget, Fake Morgan to simply stare in silence and scratch his stubble.

An outrider alongside the wagon had shouted something inaudible to teamster, Harry, who had reined the horses instantly to the left and the more open reach of the drift. Moses Barton had thrown a glowing cigar into the snow, cursed and brought his mount to within calling distance.

'Yuh want to halt?' he shouted as a handful of his sidekicks gathered closer.

'Not yet,' yelled Harry. 'I'm goin' to pull the outfit round. Wait to see just where that slide up there is comin' to rest. Ain't no point in stickin' our noses into it.'

The wagon had creaked and slithered, the horses snorted, the leather cracked and the tack jangled as the teamster slewed the outfit through a full half circle.

It had been the sight of the wagon changing direction and finally coming to a halt in the wild snow wastes that had stopped Mart Peters fidgeting and sparked him into action.

'We mount up and hit that outfit now before they got time to get organized,' he had snapped, swinging his scarf across his face. 'Let's go!'

Wilbur had tried to mouth something about the snow slide, but by then Peters was mounted and pulling clear of the boulders, gesturing for the others to follow.

Mr Coon had already reached his horse and was half-mounted when he swung round again at the sound of Wilbur's gurgled gasp.

'What the hell in the name of sanity yuh doin' there?' clicked the sidekick in a shower of saliva as he watched wide-eyed and then openmouthed as Fake Morgan's Colt steadied in his grip, levelled and in one piercing, echoing blaze blasted lead clean between Mart Peters' shoulders.

The sound of the shot roused Moses Barton's attention from the wagon. 'That you there, Fake?' he shouted. 'Finish any scum yuh got with yuh and join us here. Yuh killed Peters, sure enough. He ain't movin'. Looks as if it's all goin' just as we planned!'

23

It was the rumbling, grind and crash of the snow slide spilling across the drift that diverted Morgan's attention just long enough for Wilbur to throw his weight against the man and topple him into the boulders.

'Grab our horses there, Mr Coon,' spluttered Wilbur. 'We been sold out. This rat's tied in with Barton. We should've — '

'Fake,' yelled Barton from the wagon, 'hurry it up there, will yuh? I ain't for hangin' about longer than's necessary.'

Wilbur cursed, struggled back to his balance, reached for a loose stone and struck it violently across the back of the floundering Morgan's head. The man groaned, collapsed, dazed and bewildered again into the boulders and stayed there.

'We'd best shift,' croaked Mr Coon.

'This is gettin' decidedly unhealthy.' He handed Wilbur the reins to his mount. 'And I ain't fussed which way we ride.'

'What about the gold, damnit?' snapped Wilbur. 'Hell, we get this close, and then . . . Hell!' He mounted up and glanced quickly at Morgan. 'Who'd have figured, for it, eh? Him and Barton plannin' this from way back. And I'd reckoned for that rat, Chems Parton, bein' in on it too. Then Morgan goes and guns down Mart like that, and in the back too. For two pins I'd — '

'There ain't the time,' urged Mr Coon. 'Barton's gettin' anxious out there. And I got one helluva spooky feelin' we ain't goin' to relish one bit what's about to ride out of that snow slide when it clears . . . '

The pair had reined away, slung low and tight to their mounts' necks, back towards the sprawl of the snow-gripped peaks when Morgan finally regained his senses, wiped the smear of blood from his head and staggered from the boulders to his horse, the sounds of

Barton's shouts and curses ringing in his ears.

'Yuh fool numbskull, what yuh lettin' them scum ride out like that for? Shoot 'em! Damnit, do I have to do everythin' m'self? Why ain't there somebody, anybody . . . '

What remained of Barton's tirade was lost under the final crash and roar of the snow slide, the yells of Mr Coon and Wilbur as they urged their mounts to the thickening shadows, the jangling tack of the nervy wagon team and the murmurings of Barton's sidekicks.

'Get yourself out here, Morgan,' began Barton again. 'Harry, yuh all set then? Right, so let's get this outfit rollin'.'

A Colt blazed suddenly from the depths of the creeping dusk like the hiss and spit of unleashed flame.

There was the shape of man and horse, in one minute a stark silhouette, in the next a blur behind the rage of the shooting and the swirling cloud of snow from the slide.

Morgan's mount rose high on its hindlegs throwing the rider to the already blood-splattered snow, and for a moment the man could only stare, open-mouthed, on his knees as McGinley came on like a spectre, the Colt blazing again, tearing a wound across Morgan's chest, raising his gurgling groans until he fell forward to bury his face in the splintered ice.

McGinley reined back sharply, his gaze fixed on Moses Barton. 'And don't even think of drawing so much as a finger across that piece,' he growled. 'Same goes for the rest of you,' he called, short reining the restive mount. 'And if yuh thinkin' this is the only gun ranged against yuh, think again and take a look round yuh.'

He glanced quickly to his left to where Charley sat her mount, Colt in hand, a cold, glinting stare brightening her eyes, to his right — and this time with a gentle grin and nod of his head — as he acknowledged Mr Coon and Wilbur, guns levelled and steady.

'We ain't for sidin' along of lies and double-dealin',' clicked Wilbur before spitting long and deep. 'Yuh playin' God and the Devil, Moses Barton, and they don't bed together.'

'Where the hell did you come from, McGinley?' growled Barton, his gaze flickering anxiously from Charley, Wilbur and Mr Coon to the man facing him.

'Hell, you should know, Barton,' sniped Mr Coon. 'Yuh been drivin' him into them peaks there since yuh first set eyes on him!'

Barton sneered. 'And so now you're figurin' that a handful of guns is goin' to change everythin', eh? That it?' The sneer spread to a cynical grin. 'Three men and a two-bit whore? I think not, my friend. Why, I've only got to snap a finger to my men here and they'll be at yuh throats like a pack of mountain lions.'

'Yuh sure about that, Barton?' said McGinley. 'You explained to yuh men just what you were plannin' here?'

Barton's gaze narrowed as he shifted uncomfortably.

'Well, now, so mebbe yuh ain't at that, eh?' continued McGinley, his Colt laying easy in his grip across his lap. 'Let me surmise. Seems to me yuh been reckonin' on this heist for some time. I'd bet yuh got the first notions of it when yuh old friend, Fake Morgan, told yuh about Mart Peters' plan and how he was set to recruit Frank Boyd to his team. So what then? Yuh sent Chems Parton to kill Boyd at the cabin and get Morgan on your side. Meantime, pity I'd wandered on to the scene at Remarkable. My, my . . . Chems sure should have resisted that town and its saloon!'

McGinley paused a moment, his gaze scanning the silent, concentrated faces of Barton's sidekicks.

'And now,' smiled McGinley, 'here yuh are. All that gold and a whole heap of miners back at Johnstown who ain't never goin' to see a nugget of their sweat. Just don't seem right somehow, does it? One man puttin' his scummy hands to so much wealth. And that's what yuh plannin' on, ain't it? Keepin' the haul for yourself. Ain't a man standin' to yuh who'll be alive in a week, is there? They'll all be dead. Yuh hear that, fellas? That's the way of it with gold. Human nature don't get to smellin' one mite sweeter.'

'Think yuh smart there, don't yuh, McGinley?' mouthed Barton. 'Well, we'll see. Take him out, boys, and the others. You can have the woman for yourselves. Share her out anyway yuh fancy.'

Charley flinched and tossed her hair. Wilbur and Mr Coon stiffened, guns clenched and steady, and glanced at McGinley. But not a man at Barton's back moved a muscle.

'Yuh heard what I said,' growled Barton. 'Do it, f'Cris'sake! Now!'

McGinley stared. Charley swallowed. The sidekicks stayed silent and unmoving.

'I see,' sneered Barton, 'got to do it

m'self like I always have, eh? Same every time. Just a whole bunch of yellow-belly cowards, ain't yuh? Can't say more. Yuh make me sick! Yuh hear — yuh make me sick! But I'll show yuh. Sure I will. Just watch.'

Barton yelled, kicked his mount into action, reined tight as it pranced and rose on its hindlegs, snorting, whinnying.

'Get this, McGinley, right through yuh dumb skull!'

The single shot from Barton's gun was high and wild, a snort of flame on the deepening, snow-clouded dusk. There was no time for a second, not even the chance to steady up and take an aim, before four guns blazed as one and the mining king of Johnstown, dead before he left the saddle, slid to the frozen ground like an old, wizened hawk.

No one really knew whose shot finally killed Moses Barton.

★ ★ ★

They drove the wagon out of the Colorado mountains along the trail to Johnstown and returned the gold to its rightful owners, the majority of Barton's disillusioned sidekicks dispersing while they had the chance.

'And that, Mr Coon,' Wilbur had clicked behind a satisfied smile, 'is only fair and as it should be: the gold back where it belongs. Agreed?'

'Agreed,' his partner had nodded, ' 'specially when yuh get to countin' the reward them fellas handed out for our help and honesty. Now, ain't that somethin'?'

'Ain't I always said precisely as much, Mr Coon?'

Mr Coon could not recall a single instance of Wilbur ever referring to honesty, but had not fretted on the matter in his thoughts of their prospects out California way.

Charlotte Branham and Jim McGinley pulled out of the mining town on the first touch of a thaw and trailed quietly, peaceably to Stockburn where Charley with a 'y' established a 'gentlemen's saloon, gaming and rooming-house of taste and repute' on the proceeds of the miner's generosity and good wishes to her.

McGinley 'retired', as he put it, from his travelling life having reached the end of a long, eventful trail content in the reckoning that he had seen pretty well all it had to offer — and still survived.

He accepted the badge of sheriff of Stockburn and wed Charley one year later and has never been back to the Colorado mountains.

He can think of no good reason why he should.

THE END

We do hope that you have enjoyed reading this large print book.

Did you know that all of our titles are available for purchase?

We publish a wide range of high quality large print books including:
Romances, Mysteries, Classics
General Fiction
Non Fiction and Westerns

Special interest titles available in large print are:
The Little Oxford Dictionary
Music Book, Song Book
Hymn Book, Service Book

Also available from us courtesy of Oxford University Press:
Young Readers' Dictionary
(large print edition)
Young Readers' Thesaurus
(large print edition)

For further information or a free brochure, please contact us at:
Ulverscroft Large Print Books Ltd.,
The Green, Bradgate Road, Anstey,
Leicester, LE7 7FU, England.
Tel: (00 44) **0116 236 4325**
Fax: (00 44) **0116 234 0205**

The stage robbery had been accomplished by an old woman. Twine Fourch had never heard of a female being a highway robber before. He followed the trail all the way to a dilapidated log cabin up Stone Mountain. What happened after that no one could believe even after townsmen from Jefferson found the old log house and the skeletal dying old woman. But before the mystery could be solved there would be two unnecessary killings, a bizarre suicide and a lynching.

GUNS OF THE GAMBLER

M. Duggan

Destitute gambler Ben Crow arrives in Mallory keen to claim his inheritance, only to discover that rancher Edward Bacon has other ideas. Set up by Miss Dorothy, who had fooled him completely, Ben finds himself dangling on the end of a rope. Saved from death, Ben sets off in pursuit of Miss Dorothy, determined upon retribution. However, his quest for vengeance turns into a rescue mission when she is kidnapped by a crazy man-burning bandit.

BULLETS IN BUZZARDS CREEK

Bret Rey

The discovery of a dead saloon girl is only the beginning of Sheriff Jeff Gilpin's problems. Fortunately, his old friend 'Doc' Holliday arrives in Buzzards Creek just as Gilpin is faced by an outlaw gang. In a dramatic shoot-out the sheriff kills their leader and Holliday's reputation scares the hell out of the others. But it isn't long before the outlaws return, when they know Holliday is not around, and Gilpin is alone against six men . . .

THE YANKEE HANGMAN

Cole Rickard

Dan Tate was given a virtually impossible task: to save the murderer Jack Williams from the condemned cell. Williams, scum that he was, held a secret that was dear to the Confederate cause. But if saving Williams would test all Dan's ingenuity, then his further mission called for immense courage and daring. His life was truly on the line and if he didn't succeed, Horace Honeywell, the Yankee Hangman would have the last word!

MISSOURI PALACE

S. J. Rodgers

When ex-lawman Jim Williams accepts the post of security officer on the *Missouri Palace* riverboat, he finds himself embroiled in a power struggle between Captain J. D. Harris and Jake Farrell, the murderous boss of Willow Flats, who will stop at nothing to add the giant sidepaddler to his fleet. Williams knows that with no one to back him up in a straight fight with Farrell's hired killers, he must hit them first and hit them hard to get out alive.

THE CONRAD POSSE

Frank Scarman

The Conrad Posse, the famous group that had set about cleaning up a territory infested by human predators, was disbanding. The names of the infamous pistolmen hunted down by the Posse were now mostly a roll-call of the dead, but the name of the much sought Frank Jago was not among them. That proved to be a fatal mistake for it was not long before Jago took to his old trail of robbery and murder. Violence bred violence, and soon death stalked the land.